Murder
in
Hawthorn Road

Daphne Neville

ISBN: 978-0-244-27252-4

Publishnation
www.publishnation.co.uk

Other Titles by This Author

TRENGILLION CORNISH MYSTERY SERIES
The Ringing Bells Inn
Polquillick
Sea, Sun, Cads and Scallywags
Grave Allegations
The Old Vicarage
A Celestial Affair
Trengillion's Jubilee Jamboree

PENTRILLICK CORNISH MYSTERY SERIES
The Chocolate Box Holiday
A Pasty In A Pear Tree
The Suitcase in the Attic
Tea and Broken Biscuits
The Old Bakehouse
Death By Hanging Basket

The Old Tile House

Chapter One

All was eerily quiet in the Cornish village of Pentrillick. The faraway line between the vast ocean and the boundless sky, clearly visible in daylight, was blurred as both sides merged in a dim fuzzy haze. For across the English Channel the only lights visible were from vessels way out on the horizon, mere specks beneath the starless blanket of darkness.

Over the village the last fireworks had long faded and the houselights had gone out one by one. The roads were almost devoid of traffic for the majority of the partygoers had gone home in high spirits, their minds filled with *bonhomie* and the emotive sentiments of *Auld Lang Syne*.

Evidence of the celebrations lay scattered along Pentrillick's main street. Strands of tinsel twisted with strips of coloured paper from party poppers gathered alongside the kerbs or fluttered in the gentle breeze from fences, gateposts and hedgerows. Meanwhile, its string free from the constraints of obstacles in its path, a solitary white balloon bearing the message *A Happy New Year* bounced beneath the swaying Christmas lights. It danced along the pavement, past the village hall, and when it reached the church, its bells now silent having rung in the year 2020, it stopped, caught on a bench near to the lichgate steps illuminated by bright pearl light bulbs draped amongst the branches of an elderly yew tree. The balloon's entrapment was brief and brought to an end by the draught from a passing taxi. Freed from the bench it continued on its way towards the Old Bakehouse where a breeze blew up from the sea and sent it spinning into Goose Lane. With the wind behind it, it tumbled and swirled along the road, bouncing off parked cars as it made its way up the steep hill and into Hawthorn Road where it bobbed along the tops of hedgerows before finally coming to rest in the lower branches of a lilac tree in the front garden of number thirteen where a ginger tom cat was keeping watch for a small rodent he sensed to be amongst the undergrowth.

Inside the Crown and Anchor, licensees James and Ella Dale busily tidied up the bar, the last of the revellers having long gone home. They were helped by their son, Harry, home from university for the festive season and members of staff, Tess Dobson and Jackie Paige. All five, dressed as characters from Alice in Wonderland, yawned, bleary eyed and weary after a long and busy night pouring drinks for the villagers who had packed the pub to its full capacity.

"I bet you'll be glad to get back to uni, won't you, Harry?" James asked, "We've worked you rather hard this holiday."

"Yeah, but I've enjoyed it. It's gone really quick and I've made a few new friends too."

"When do you go back?" Tess knelt down to recover an empty glass she had just spotted beneath the Christmas tree.

"The day after tomorrow so I've worked my last session now."

Ella, dressed as the Queen of Hearts, sat down and removed her crown. "That's it. I think we've tidied enough. The glasses are all washed, the bar counter's clean and we've brushed up all the party popper strands and whistles."

James cast his eyes around the bar. "I suppose you're right and we need to leave something for the cleaner to do in the morning."

Ella looked at her watch. "And that'll be soon. It's already four so she'll be here in five hours."

"Has anyone cleared the glasses and party poppers in the dining room?" Tess glanced at the closed door, her fingers crossed.

Harry raised his hand. "Yep me."

"Brilliant, well done. Can I get off home now then?"

"Yes, of course, off you go and you too, Jackie. I need to get out of this ridiculous costume and put my feet up for a while to unwind before bed." James rubbed his hand across his stomach where thick padding lay beneath a colourful tunic.

"You don't look ridiculous at all," Tess reached from a shelf over the bar for her handbag, "In fact you look rather fetching as Tweedledum and your outfit certainly made people smile."

"Maybe, but I think next year we'll opt for something where I can be a bit more macho. Rosy cheeks isn't really my thing."

Jackie slipped on her coat and then removed the blonde wig she had worn all evening as Alice. Harry laughed and pointed to her hair as she pushed the wig into her bag. For its usual gelled spikes were flattened and her short black hair was a mess. Intrigued by his ridicule, Jackie looked in the mirror behind the bar and promptly replaced the wig. "I think this is the lesser of the two evils."

"Oh, don't say that. I thought how pretty you looked in the wig," said Ella, "Please don't get me wrong because I'm not criticising your spikes it's just I think longer hair suits you better."

Tess nodded. "I agree but then Ella and I being in our forties are out of touch I suppose."

"No, you're not out of touch. Far from it." Jackie looked again at herself in the mirror. "Actually, I think you're right and it is a nice length but I should hate to be blonde."

"Is black your natural colour?" Ella asked.

"I wish. No, it's a miserable non-descript light brown." Jackie pulled on a pair of leather gloves, "Anyway, I need to go now before I fall asleep on my feet. Are you ready, Tess?"

Tess zipped up her jacket. "I am," she gave everyone a hug, "see you all tomorrow."

James unlocked the door to let them out. "Goodnight, girls, and thank you for working so hard. You're both stars."

As James locked the front door, Harry poured himself a glass of water, said goodnight to his parents and went upstairs to his room.

"Well that's our first Christmas and New Year's Eve here done and dusted," said Ella, "and what a success it's been."

"It has, it's been brilliant and I've really enjoyed it," James sat down beside his wife and took her hand. "We did the right thing, didn't we, Ella? Coming here to Pentrillick, I mean."

"We did. It's a smashing place and the people are wonderful and what good sports they were to dress up tonight."

New Year's Day dawned mild and damp. Inside Primrose Cottage, Lottie rose a little later than usual to find Hetty was already up and had the multi fuel fire burning brightly.

"That's a welcome sight. I must admit I feel a bit fragile this morning. I don't think late nights agree with me."

"Me neither so I'm not sorry it only comes round once a year. Having said that, it was a really enjoyable evening."

"It was. Anyway, I'm making tea so would you like another, Het?"

"Yes, please. I'm really thirsty this morning. Serves me right, I should have drunk some water before I went to bed." Hetty picked up her empty mug from the hearth and passed it to her sister. She then put another log on the fire.

"I see the hyacinths are flowering at last," Lottie called from the kitchen.

"Are they?" Hetty went to take a look, "Well, I'll be blowed. I didn't notice. I'll put them in the sitting room now then so they can benefit from the sun, should it ever shine again." She glanced out of the kitchen window and cast a disparaging look at the damp paving slabs beneath the washing line.

Lottie poured boiling water into two mugs. "Pity they weren't in flower for Christmas. Not that it mattered because the poinsettia's been a picture these last few weeks. I think everyone who's seen it has complimented it."

"They have, but it'll be nice to have an extra bit of colour now it's January because things always look a bit drab when the decorations come down." Hetty picked up the bowl containing six hyacinths and carried it into the sitting room where she placed it on the window sill beside the praiseworthy poinsettia.

"What are you going to do with your fancy dress costume?" Lottie placed the two mugs of tea on the coffee table.

"Take it back to the charity shop I suppose but I'll wash it first."

"I'll do the same as I'm unlikely to want to dress as Little Bo-Peep again." Lottie sat down on the sofa. "I think dressing up as characters from nursery rhymes or children's books was a brilliant idea, don't you? So ten out of ten to whoever thought of it."

"I agree and I was really impressed with the effort some people went to."

Lottie took a sip of tea and then leaned back into the cushions. "I can't believe we've reached 2020 already. It seems like only yesterday that we were welcoming in the new millennium."

"Oh dear. So that means the London Eye and the Millennium Dome thing are twenty years old now. That's ridiculous! I really don't know where the last twenty years have gone," Hetty groaned, "and I've just realised we would only have been forty-seven back then."

"Forty-seven! That was a really nice age. Bill and Barbara had grown up and the mortgage on our house was nearing its end."

"And I was still working back then of course. Oh happy days. Not that I'm unhappy now, in fact far from it."

"But you just wish the time would slow down a bit." Lottie finished her tea and placed the empty mug back on the coffee table.

"I do, but at least with this year being a leap year we'll get an extra day. Every little helps as they say."

"It's leap year, is it? I didn't realise that."

"Yes, I always remember because it coincides with the Olympic Games which are of course every four years the same."

"Well, you learn something every day." Lottie looked at the Christmas tree where a wishbone painted silver caught the light from the flames in the fire, "I wonder what this year holds for us. Last year the pub changed hands and was refurbished, Vicar Sam got married and so along with many other things it was quite eventful."

"I think it's best not to know. I just hope we're all still here in a year's time. You know, family friends and associates."

"That's a morbid thought but I have to agree."

"So, have you come up with a New Year's resolution yet, Lottie?"

"No, I think I've been through them all over the years and doubt that I ever stuck to any of them. Have you?"

"Yes, I have. When we go to the pub I'm going to limit myself to just two glasses of wine a night. I might even drink tonic water occasionally."

"Lottie laughed. "You won't manage that for a month let alone a year."

"I think you might be surprised."

"Shocked more like. That reminds me, did you see the notice in the pub saying they're going to start having a weekly quiz night on Sunday evenings?"

Hetty shook her head. "No, I didn't but what a good idea. Be nice to get the old grey matter working. When's the first one?"

"Not sure. I saw it when I went to the Ladies and was going to tell you but with all the noise it slipped my mind."

"Well, whenever it is I think it's a brilliant idea and something else to add to our diaries. It all helps pass the dark days of winter."

"And it'll make up for the fact there are no Gardening Club meetings now 'til February."

Remembering that she had taken pictures inside the pub on New Year's Eve, Hetty reached for her phone and chuckled as she scrolled through her efforts. "Ah, there's Zac's mate Dodge. He seemed a nice lad and I think he made a brilliant Harry Potter."

"He did. I chatted with him for a while and he said how glad he was to have finally made it to Cornwall. He and Emma got on really well, which is nice for Zac."

"Well, I daresay Dodge has heard lots about her over the years. As we all know, Zac's besotted with her." Hetty passed her phone to Lottie so that she could see the pictures.

"They're very good, Het, and that one of Zac and Emma is lovely." She looked up: "It's just struck me that Zac's so grown up now yet twenty years ago when we all welcomed in the year 2000, he wasn't even born."

Chapter Two

Lottie's grandson, Zac, worked with Sid Moore, a plumber with whom he was doing an apprenticeship. Their work took them to all sorts of homes and businesses in the area and their first job after the Christmas/New Year holiday was at a house in Hawthorn Road where they had been called in to fit a new bathroom suite.

The house had originally belonged to the local authorities and was sold to the then tenants in the early nineteen eighties. After changing hands several times it was eventually bought by the current owners, Vivien Spencer and her husband, Graham. The purpose of their purchase was to rent it out. This they had done for two years but now it was empty, for their first and only tenant, Nigel Taylor, had collapsed in a supermarket carpark just before Christmas following a heart attack where despite efforts to save him he had died before he reached the hospital.

After looking over the property, Vivien and Graham decided to have the bathroom refurbished before they sought another tenant as it looked rather careworn. Some of the tiles were cracked, the suite was outdated and its taps were corroded. To oversee the work, Vivien decided that after Christmas she would stay at the house while the project was ongoing rather than travel back and forth between Pentrillick and her home in Devon; while she was there she would be able to look for any further improvements that might enhance the property.

Monday January the sixth was Sid and Zac's first day working after the Christmas and New Year break. However, they had already met Vivien and Graham Spencer briefly when they had visited the house on Christmas Eve to price up the job before the Spencers returned to Devon for the festive season.

When they arrived for work, Vivien warmly welcomed them to number thirteen Hawthorn Road. The house struck warm and in the sitting room a coal fire burned in the hearth. "Good morning, lads. Did you both have a lovely Christmas?"

Sid nodded. "Yes, and as usual I ate and drank too much."

Zac smiled. "We had a lovely time too, thanks. It was the first time Em and me were able to spend Christmas together in our own place, and my old school friend Dodge came down from up-country to see in the New Year with us so that was fantastic."

"So, did you see in the New Year here in the village?"

"Yes, at the Crown and Anchor," enthused Zac, "It was brilliant and ideal too as it meant no expensive taxi fares."

"I've heard it's a nice pub, but we've never actually been in there. Perhaps I should give it a try while I'm here."

Sid removed his scarf. "You should. I'm quite a regular. Perhaps too much of a regular but then why not?"

"How about you, Mrs Spencer?" Zac asked, "Did you have a nice Christmas?"

"Vivien please, and yes we did. Graham and I had a quiet time and actually went out for dinner on Christmas Day. It was nice but I think next year, or should I say this year, we'll stay at home and then we can put our feet up and watch the telly without having to get dressed up and leave the house. I must admit I don't really like going out in the winter muffled up in coats, scarves and so forth."

Sid chuckled. "Same here but I was lucky because I went next door for dinner with my mates Bernie and Veronica. It was smashing especially as I didn't have to walk too far."

After the brief exchange of festive talk, Sid and Zac went upstairs to start work. An hour later, Vivien called them down for a break when she gave them coffee and Christmas cake.

"I see you have a visitor now," Sid nodded towards a ginger cat lazing on the rug by the fire.

"Yes, that's Oscar. He belonged to Nigel, our erstwhile tenant. Susan and Tim Rudd who live next door have adopted him but he still keeps coming back round here because he likes the fire. They don't have one, you see. They had it bricked up thirty years ago when they had central heating installed. Both were working back then and so wanted instant heat when they got home. They've retired now though."

"Yes, I know the couple you mean. We installed an outside tap for them last summer because they intended to get into gardening now they have time on their hands."

Zac sat down. "So does Oscar come round and knock on the door?"

"No, he comes in through the cat flap. Bless him."

"Cheeky bugger," chuckled Sid, "Still, I can't say as I blame him. I like to see an open fire even if they are inefficient."

"Did you know Nigel at all?" Vivien knelt down on the hearth rug and stroked Oscar's soft fur coat, "I meant to ask you when we met before the Christmas holiday but completely forgot."

Sid shook his head. "I can't say that I did. Had he lived here long?"

"Not really. No more than a couple of years."

"Any idea what he did?" Sid took a large bite of cake.

"No, I don't actually but he always paid his rent on time and was no trouble at all."

Vivien glanced around the room. "I think since we're having the bathroom done we might as well go the whole hog, clear everything out and give the place a thorough makeover. I mentioned it to Graham when we looked the place over before

Christmas and he seemed to think it might be a good idea. If we did we could let it out unfurnished next time as I know a lot of people like to have their own things around them especially if they're going to stay for some time."

"So are the contents here all yours then?" Sid patted the arm of the chair in which he sat beside the fire.

"Yes, they are. When we purchased the house a couple years ago we bought its contents too. The vendor's elderly mother who lived here had died or it might even have been a father, anyway, whatever they didn't want anything other than their parents' personal things like photos, jewellery and so forth. As Graham and I were buying the place solely to rent out we reasoned to have the contents left here was the obvious thing to do. But as you can see some of the furniture is looking a bit shabby now and the paint on the walls is discoloured in places."

"You'll have to have an auction here then," said Sid, "events like that are always popular."

"Hmm, we might even do that but I'll need to go through things first as of course not everything in here is ours. Clothes, toiletries and stuff like that obviously belonged to Nigel and I'm not sure what to do with it all. He and his family weren't close, you see. In fact, I believe they'd not been in touch for years. They're dealing with his finances and so forth, but they want nothing from the house. Fortunately, Nigel's tenancy agreement ran out at the end of the year. We would have renewed it automatically had he wished but now of course it's not to be. It's really sad, his family don't even want to come and see what little he had. Although I suppose it's hardly worth their while to come down just to look over a few old clothes."

"You could always take the best clothes to the charity shop. I'm sure the ladies would appreciate it and it's all for a good cause."

11

"Now that's an excellent idea, I'll do that and take any unused toiletries as well. As regards everything else though, I think rather than go to the hassle of bringing in an auctioneer and putting everything into Lots, we'll just give it all away. After all it cost us next to nothing. In fact, I've made up my mind that's what we'll do. I'll bag Nigel's clothes up and take them to the charity shop. Meanwhile if there's anything here that takes your fancy please help yourselves. Not Nigel's mobile phone and laptop though. I've yet to decide what to do with them." She glanced to where both lay on top of an old-fashioned writing bureau.

Zac's eyes lit up. "When you say anything do you mean absolutely anything?"

Vivien laughed. "Of course. Everything must go as they say in closing down sales, except of course the bed I'm sleeping in at the moment and the kitchen appliances because I need to cook and eat but even they can go when I'm ready to go home."

Sid finished his piece of cake and placed the empty plate on the coffee table. "Young Zac here and his girlfriend moved into one of the houses on the new estate a couple of months ago so they're still getting things together."

"Ideal then. Please, Zac, take whatever you want."

"Wow! Thank you and I know it's cheeky, but can I have your bed when you've finished with it? As I said earlier, my best mate Dodge came down to visit us for a couple of days over the New Year and he had to sleep on the sofa because we don't have a bed in our spare room."

"Consider it yours, Zac and you must have all the bedding too. It's a nice bed and unlike most of the other things here it's only a couple of years old. We bought a new one, you see, because the old one was ancient. It had springs and some were broken," she chuckled, "It looked like it came out of the ark."

"That's brilliant, thank you so much. Emma will be dead chuffed."

Vivien smiled sweetly, delighted to see such a small offering had made a young man very happy. "With any luck we'll have finished everything here by the end of the month and you can take the bed and so forth away then. Meanwhile, as I said, if there's anything here you want to take away today, please help yourself."

"Hmm, that might be a problem as the van's chock-a-block at the moment," said Sid, "but I'll take out what's not needed for this job tonight and then we can load up whatever stuff this young man wants tomorrow if that's alright with you."

"Sounds fine. Meanwhile I'll chuck out things that are no good to anyone and then after I've bagged up Nigel's clothes for the charity shop, I'll start cleaning the kitchen. Fortunately, that's in quite good order as we had new units fitted before poor Nigel moved in here." She glanced towards the window where grey clouds were visibly rolling in from the west, "On the other hand I really ought to do a spot of gardening before the next lot of rain gets here. Perhaps I can find time to do that later. As you probably noticed the front's very untidy: the gateposts are covered in ivy and there's a deflated balloon caught in the lower branches of the lilac tree. When Nigel moved in I asked him if he'd like us to get someone to come in and keep the garden tidy but he said no, he'd do it himself."

"He obviously didn't have green fingers," Sid stood up and pointed to his empty plate, "That Christmas cake's delicious, by the way. Did you make it yourself?"

"I did but I don't really know why as neither Graham nor I have a sweet tooth."

"Lucky you then, that's always been my weakness."

"I was hoping that might be the case and that's why I brought it with me from home," Vivien stood and collected the empty mugs and plates, "While I think of it, do you know anyone who does decorating? I'm not meaning anything elaborate, but I'd like to see the walls painted white to freshen the place up a bit. I'd do it myself but I'm not very good at standing on ladders even when it's only a foot off the floor."

Sid rubbed his chin. "No-one springs to mind."

"How about Norman?" said Zac, "Dad told me he's going to do decorating and stuff like that for a few years until he gets his old age pension. He'd probably tidy the garden as well if you wanted him to."

"Of course, I'd forgotten Norman," Sid turned to Vivien, "He's new to the village, you see, and has bought one of the houses on the new estate. Having said that, he's not really new because we've known him for a year or so and he was born in the village but that's another story as they say."

Norman Williams finished laying a carpet in the spare bedroom and then stood back to admire his handiwork. Pleased with the result he called downstairs to Jackie and asked for her opinion. Jackie ran up the stairs and peeped round the doorjamb. "Wow, it's looking fantastic and it's taken you less than two hours. Well done."

Norman beamed with pride. "Yep. Mind you it was easy enough with straight walls and no nooks, crannies and fireplaces to deal with. I must admit I'm dead chuffed and it's not bad for an old man of sixty-three is it?"

Jackie punched his arm. "Old man indeed! You might have a few wrinkles but you're young at heart and have a positive outlook in life."

"Yeah, I like to think that's the case. Anyway, what are we going to put in here?"

Jackie shrugged her shoulders. "A bed, I suppose. I mean that's normally what people put in their spare bedrooms."

"Yes, I know that but what sort? I mean, are we going to have a double, a single, bunk beds or what?"

"Oh, I see what you mean." Jackie stepped into the room. "We don't want bunkbeds because we're not likely to have children to stay and they're a pig to make anyway. I think it might be best if we went for two singles."

"Do you think there's room?"

"Yeah, should be. I mean there won't be much else in here, will there?"

"A chest of drawers I suppose and perhaps a wardrobe. We'll see how much room when we've got a couple of beds in."

Jackie walked over to the widow. "Nice view of the estate from here. Ideal for anyone who likes to spy on their neighbours."

"Hmm, it'd suit several ladies in the village then."

"Who shall remain nameless." Jackie looked at her watch. "Anyway, I need to get to work. We've a party of twelve coming in this lunchtime for a ninetieth birthday."

"That sounds fun."

"You might be surprised. Since I've been working in the pub I've been quite astounded by the behaviour of some of the village's senior citizens although none of them are anywhere near ninety yet."

"Yes, I can believe that. And I've just remembered what I was thinking when I woke up this morning. It's we need to come up with a name for this place. I think it deserves more than just a number, don't you?"

"Absolutely. I'll put my thinking cap on while I'm working and then we'll discuss it later."

Jackie Paige was Norman's twenty-three-year-old lodger. Previously they had been next-door neighbours in Dawlish where Jackie lived with her parents and Norman lived with his elderly widowed mother. They became good friends when

15

Jackie and her mother helped Norman to look after his mother in the last months of her life. It was after his mother's death that Norman looked into his past and Jackie who had an interest in ancestry had helped him. This led them to Pentrillick where Norman discovered his Cornish roots. With no family left in Dawlish after his mother's demise there was little to keep him in Devon and so after much deliberation, he decided to take early retirement and return to the county of his birth. Since Jackie had made friends in the village during their investagitive visit she asked if she might go with him as a paying lodger.

They moved into the house on the new estate just before Christmas and straight away Jackie secured a job at the Crown and Anchor where she assisted the chef or worked on the bar. Norman meanwhile, decided to do a bit of painting and decorating. It was something he enjoyed and was good at.

When Jackie left the house to go to work she saw the next door neighbours, Polly and Jay Digsby out in their front garden.

"Ah, you're back. Did you have a lovely Christmas?"

Polly's face exuded enthusiasm. "Lovely, thanks, Jackie, but the two weeks just flew by."

"I bet. So when did you get back?"

"Last night around one, wasn't it, Jay?"

"Bit later than that. I remember hearing the church clock strike two as I took the luggage from the car."

"Well, whatever, you must have been very quiet because I didn't hear you but then my room's on the back of the house so I suppose I wouldn't have heard the car."

"We did try to be quiet."

Jay tucked his hands into the pocket of his jacket. "So did anything exciting happen while we were away?" Other than Christmas of course."

"No, not really. In fact apart from Christmas and the fact the pub was heaving on New Year's Eve, the only thing I can think of is that some poor chap died just before the holiday."

"Oh dear, that's sad. Anyone we know?" Polly asked.

"Not sure. I didn't know him but I think his name was Nigel. Yes that's right, Nigel Taylor. I remember the Taylor bit because an old friend of mine had that surname before she married."

"So what happened to the poor chap?" Polly asked, "I mean, was it natural causes?"

"Yes, apparently he had a heart attack while out shopping. He was only fifty-three."

"Fifty-three," gasped Polly, "but that's terrible. Poor, poor man."

"Where did this Nigel Taylor live?" Jay asked.

"Somewhere along Hawthorn Road wherever that might be. I only know the main part of the village," Jackie admitted.

"Same with us," said Polly, "I keep meaning to go exploring but haven't got round to it yet."

"Well, it'll be something to do when the weather improves," Jackie looked at the threatening grey clouds, "that's if it ever does."

Jay rolled his eyes.

"Was this Nigel chap married?" Polly hoped his death had not left any children fatherless.

"I don't think so. He lived alone so I assume he was a bachelor."

"Or a divorcee," Jay added.

"Could be," said Polly, "but whatever, it just goes to show that you never can be sure of seeing tomorrow."

"That's so very true," Jackie noticed a spade by Jay's side. "Bit miserable for gardening, isn't it?" The thought caused her to wrap her scarf snuggly around her neck.

"It is," said Polly, "and there's heavy rain forecast, but Mum and Dad bought us this gorgeous camellia while we were up there for Christmas. Dad said they do well down here because they like the soil and so we want to get it planted in case the weather turns really cold. I noticed there were lots of berries on the holly in late autumn and my gran always vowed that meant we were in for a hard winter."

Jay glanced at their front garden. "The problem is, at the moment we're not quite sure where to put it as they can grow quite large."

"Well, it has to be either here by the gate or in the corner," said Polly, "we certainly don't want it too near the house as it might block out the light."

Jackie stepped out onto the pavement. "Put it near the gate and then Norman and me can see it too."

"Yes, I think I'd prefer it there too," said Polly, "then we'll be able to see it from all of our front windows."

"Right, problem solved." Jay moved towards the gate, plunged the spade into the wet earth and began to dig a suitably sized hole.

Jackie gave the couple the thumbs up. "Yay, brilliant, I look forward to seeing it when I get back from work."

From an upstairs window, Jackie caught sight of Barnaby, a young rescue dog Jay had given to Polly shortly after they had moved into the house. "You have a spectator," she laughed, as she turned to walk out of newly named Cobblestone Close.

"You little perisher. How did you get up there? You know the bedroom's out of bounds." Polly abandoned the garden and ran indoors to remove Barnaby from the window sill, Jay continued to dig and Jackie continued on her way to the Crown and Anchor.

Chapter Three

When Sid and Zac went to work on Tuesday morning, Vivien told them that she had rung her husband the previous evening and he was very enthusiastic about giving everything away, so she reiterated her statement saying they were welcome to take away anything they liked.

Sid put down a box of tools. "Ideal, because I've got quite a bit of room in the van now. In fact loads of room. I didn't realise just how much junk I've been carrying around."

"Excellent, well when you're ready, please help yourself," Vivien pulled back the curtains and looked out of the window, "In fact it might be as well to do it now as it looks like we might be in for some more rain."

As Zac collected a few things together, Sid nodded towards the window. "I noticed when we came in that you didn't get round to pulling the ivy off the gateposts."

"No, I didn't. Still, never mind, I'll get it done one day. In fact, I might even get your Norman to do it if he's able to do the painting."

"I'm sure he will and it pays to prioritise anyway," Sid chuckled, "and let's face it, nobody bothers much with their gardens this time of the year. I haven't touched mine since September."

"Same with us back home," agreed Vivien, "but then so far this has been an exceptionally wet winter."

"It certainly has and going back to your gatepost, I think you might need a new one anyway. I looked at it closely when we got here this morning and it's quite rotten in places."

"Even better then. If we replace it we'll be able to get the ivy roots out. If a job's worth doing it's worth doing well."

"My motto exactly."

"I'm pleased to hear it, Sid," Vivien glanced at the ceiling where Zac's footsteps could be heard on the upstairs landing, "Tell Zac if he needs any boxes there are several in the kitchen. Meanwhile, I'll go and put the kettle on."

"In that case I'll grab a couple now because I'm sure the lad will need them."

With boxes in hand, Sid went to see how Zac was doing and found he had several things standing by the front door including a huge pile of books. "You like reading then."

"They're for Grandma and Auntie Hetty," Zac stepped into the hallway with a mirror from the spare bedroom, "They often have their heads stuck in books especially in the winter so I thought they might like them although I'm not sure whether they like military thrillers and there are quite a few of them."

Sid looked through the books. "Maybe not in which case I know someone who would appreciate them and that's Norman. He and I were chatting in the pub only the other night and he said then that military thrillers were his favourite genre."

"Ideal."

"So shall I take them out and leave the rest for you to take to the good ladies."

"Yeah, why not. Then when you've done that I'll pack up the rest."

"Have you told Emma about this stuff?" Sid began to sort the books into two piles.

"No and I'm looking forward to seeing her face when she sees it. I decided not to tell her because I wanted it to be a surprise."

"Well, I hope she likes what you've chosen."

"So do I, but it's not a problem if she doesn't, is it? I mean, anything she dislikes I can give to Mum or Gran or even the charity shop."

"Coffee's ready," Vivien called from the kitchen, "Get yourselves sitting by the fire and I'll bring it in."

After Sid and Zac had drunk coffee and eaten more Christmas cake, Vivien reached for her coat. "Right, I'm popping out now for a while to take bags of Nigel's clothes to the charity shop and then I'm going to the supermarket. If I'm not back before you stop for lunch please feel free to help yourselves to tea or coffee."

"Thank you very much," said Sid, "You take care and we'll see you later."

Emma was already home on Tuesday afternoon when she heard Sid's van stop outside just after five to drop off Zac. She promptly put on the kettle to make them both tea; as the kettle came to the boil she realised Zac had not entered the house. Wondering where he might be, she went to front door and looked outside. To her amazement, Zac and Sid were unloading all sorts of things from the back of Sid's van. To improve visibility, she switched on the outside light.

"Don't be mad with me, Em but this is for us if we want it. Vivien who owns the house we're working in is going to give the place a makeover and she said we can take away anything we want for free."

Emma kissed Zac's cheek. "Mad, why would I be mad?" She picked up a vase. "I was only saying the other day we've nothing to put flowers in and this looks gorgeous."

Sid looked to the sky. "Better get this inside quick as it looks to me like we're in for some more rain."

Once everything was indoors, Sid left for his home in Honeysuckle Drive after saying he'd pick Zac up at seven thirty the next day as usual.

"There's loads more if we want it, Em, including furniture, electrical things and crockery and I've reserved us a double bed too for our spare room but we can't have it yet because Vivien's sleeping in it. It's really nice, only two years old and we can have the bedding to go with it too. In fact, I think it might be a good idea if you popped round one day to take a look while we're working there. Vivien won't mind, in fact she suggested it as we were leaving just now. She wants everything gone, you see."

"I'll do that on Friday then as it's my day off." Emma pulled aside a vacuum cleaner, "This is very nice but we don't really need two though, do we?"

"Ah, no. Well I was actually thinking of taking that up to Primrose Cottage. When I was there the other day, Grandma muttered something about the vacuum cleaner being on its last legs. I thought Vivien might want to keep it to do the carpets at number thirteen but she said she doesn't. She has two at her house in Devon, you see, and she's intending to bring her favourite back with her when she pops home at the weekend. It's cordless apparently and she prefers that. The books are for Grandma and Auntie Het too as they're both fond of reading."

"Ideal then. We'll take them up to them this evening."

"Yes, I thought that but better not leave it too late though because it's bingo tonight and they do like their bingo."

Emma looked at the clock. "In that case we'll have a cup of tea then pop up there before we have dinner."

"I suppose now we've passed twelfth night they'll be taking down the Christmas lights at the weekend," sighed Hetty, "The road seems awfully dark without them despite the streetlamps."

Lottie cast a glance at the dark strings of lights swaying in the breeze. "It does. Roll on summer."

Hetty groaned. "Oh, don't say that. I know the winter can be tiresome but we've another birthday before summer and they're coming round too fast as it is. I really don't relish the idea of being sixty-eight. It's far too close to seventy."

Inside the village hall they met up with their friend, Debbie Elms, a lady of a similar age to themselves. They played several games, Debbie even won one of them, and then afterwards they made their usual visit to the Crown and Anchor. As they had hoped, the table near to the fireplace was free so they removed their coats and sat down. Hetty then went to the bar for three glasses of red wine.

"Zac and Emma came round today with a vacuum cleaner and a box of books from the house where Zac and Sid are working in Hawthorn Road," said Hetty, as she returned with the drinks and sat down, "You know, Nigel Taylor's place. Not that we knew him."

Debbie nodded. "Yes, Lottie was just telling me. He's the poor chap who had a heart attack, isn't he? I never met him either but Gideon told me he was only in his fifties."

"Fifty-three, according to Zac," said Lottie.

Hetty tutted. "No age at all."

Debbie took a sip of wine. "So how come Zac got a vacuum cleaner and books from there? Lottie didn't get as far as telling me that."

Hetty loosened her scarf. "Because Vivien whatever she's called and her husband who own the place want to give the house a makeover before they put in more tenants and so they're giving everything away so they can start from fresh."

"Everything. That's a bit extreme, isn't it?"

"No, because they're going to let it out unfurnished next time." Lottie stood down her glass of wine and then reached into her handbag for her purse. "I'm feeling a bit peckish so I'm going to get some crisps."

"Probably the cold weather," said Hetty, "it always makes me hungry."

Debbie groaned. "Me too. Every year I put on half a stone during the winter months. Mind you, it doesn't help that we always have boxes of chocolates and tins of toffees to get through in January that we've been given for Christmas."

"Yuck, it's best not to think about weight," laughed Hetty, "especially at our age when there's no-one to impress."

"Oh, that's a depressing thought."

"Yes, but sadly it's true. I've heard it said many times that senior ladies are invisible to the younger generation and especially men. Although I'm sure your Gideon still has eyes for you, Debs."

"I hope so and he's very sweet. He never comments when I put on a few pounds or look a mess."

"Good. Anyway, where were we?"

"You were saying about Vivien thingy giving things away."

"That's right, yes. Well I was going to say that she and her husband have got plenty of money so they can afford to give stuff away. I know that because Tess Dobson told me when she was saying about poor Nigel Taylor having died. Apparently the two of them own thirty-eight properties in the South West and they have tenants in them all."

"Thirty-eight!" Debbie's jaw dropped.

"Yep, thirty-eight."

"Humph, alright for some."

"It is and I've just remembered Vivien's surname. It's Spencer not that we really need to know that because we'll probably never even see her."

At the bar Lottie stood near to Norman who sat on a barstool.

"You're a lady of good taste," he said, "what do you think of the names 'Early Dawn' and 'Sunrise'? For a house that is."

"They're both nice providing you can see the sun from the windows."

"Oh damn, we hadn't thought of that and we can't see the sunrise because of the trees in the lane."

"I assume then that you're trying to think of a name for your place?"

"Yes, we are. I don't like just being a number but thinking of one's really difficult." Norman absentmindedly ran his finger through the condensation on his glass of beer which caused it to squeak.

Lottie chuckled. "Well in that case I think 'Early Dawn' and 'Sunrise' are not really appropriate, are they?"

"No. It's driving us mad, you know. Jackie and I have spent ages trying to come up with something but we feel a bit limited. I mean, the place is too new for it to be something cottage and it's not big enough to be something house."

"Have Jay and Polly named their place?"

"Yes, they've called it 'Rainbows End'."

"Ow, I like that."

"So do we. I wish we'd thought of it first."

"How about planting something in the front garden and then naming after that. You, know, the Cedars, the Pines, the Lilacs or something like that."

Norman chuckled. "That's not a bad idea because at the moment it's just grass. Jay and Polly have planted a camellia in their front garden and it's improved the look of the place no end. I'll see what Jackie says when she finishes work because she likes gardening."

"We planted our Christmas tree today. We had one with roots on, you see. It's quite small and we don't know whether or not it'll survive but it's worth a try."

Norman's face lit up. "Now, that's an idea. Ours has roots on too. At the moment it's standing in its pot outside the back door but I'll plant it tomorrow."

Lottie bought three bags of crisps and returned to the table.

"Are they for us?" Hetty's eyes lit up.

"Yes, I know you didn't ask for them but it's bound to make you hungry when I start crunching and I can't have you pinching mine."

"Thank you," said Debbie, "Salt and Vinegar too. My favourites."

Lottie sat back down. "I've been talking to Norman. He and Jackie are trying to come up with a name for their house and it's driving them mad. Polly and Jay have called their place 'Rainbow's End' and Norman wishes they'd thought of it first."

"We saw you talking to him," Hetty opened her bag of crisps, "So has he come up with any ideas?"

"No, only 'Sunrise' and 'Early Dawn'. Neither is any good though because they can't see the sun rise from their place because of some trees."

"If it was mine I'd call it 'Spinneyside'," said Debbie: "something like that anyway as they're only a stone's throw away from the spinney."

Hetty nodded. "Yes, I think anything to do with flowers, trees and the countryside is popular."

Seeing Lottie beckon him over, Norman picked up his glass and joined the ladies.

"Sit down," said Lottie, "and we'll all try to come up with a name."

"I wish you would because we're both at our wits' end."

Hetty chuckled. "There you are then 'Wits' End'. Perfect name."

"What!" Norman seemed confused.

"Absolutely," said Lottie, "'Rainbow's End' and 'Wits' End'. Ideal for two houses side by side at the top of a close."

A broad smile crept across Norman's face. "Oh, I see what you mean. Thank you so much, ladies. That's a huge weight off my mind and I just know Jackie will love it. Mr Norman Williams, 'Wits' End', 17, Cobblestone Close, Pentrillick. Perfect."

"Why have they named the estate Cobblestone Close? I've been meaning to ask for ages," said Debbie.

"Because it's a straight road with houses on either side and then there's a big banjo at the end and in the centre of the banjo is a raised circular area of beautifully laid out cobbles with an old fashioned looking streetlamp bang in the middle," said Norman. "It's really nice."

"I see, and whereabouts in the close is your house?"

"At the top of the banjo in the middle, and so from the upstairs front windows we have a lovely view right down the close."

Chapter Four

It was wet, windy and still dark on Wednesday morning when Sid picked up Zac at seven thirty. Zac, who had waited outside in the front porch for his lift, shivered as he climbed into Sid's van.

"Bloomin' horrible out there today. I'm glad we're working indoors."

"Me too and I'm looking forward to another slice of that Christmas cake."

Zac placed his lunchbox in the footwell and then fastened his seat belt. "That's if Vivien hasn't eaten it all."

"No, she won't have done that. Remember she said she and her husband didn't really like cake because neither have a sweet tooth."

Zac laughed. "I don't see how anyone can dislike cake."

Sid released the handbrake and drove out of the estate. "So, what did Emma think of the stuff?"

"She was thrilled to bits and she's coming up to Hawthorn Road on Friday to see what else we need. Grandma and Auntie Het were dead chuffed with the vacuum cleaner too."

Sid chuckled. "I hope it works alright. Judging by the state of the carpet in the hallway at number thirteen I'd say Nigel either wasn't very domesticated or it's a duff."

"They switched it on and it sounded okay. Grandma said she'll look at it properly today as they were just about to have dinner before they went off to bingo last night. They were thrilled to bits with the books too and said if no-one wants it they'll have the bookcase as well because they've a place for it to go in their dining room. I also told them about the writing bureau but as much as they liked the idea there's nowhere really they could put it."

"We'll take the bookcase up later then but as regards the bureau I'd mention that to your mum and dad if I were you as it'd be in keeping with their old place."

"Good thinking, I'll do that. I mean the more we can get out the easier it'll be for Norman to paint."

"Assuming he gets the job," said Sid. "I don't think Vivien's asked him yet. But then she probably wants more stuff gone before she does."

"So did the table lamp you took fit on the shelf like you hoped?

"It did and it's a perfect match with my curtains too. I must admit that's pure coincidence as I'd never given colour a thought. I don't expect she'll take it because she's not short of a bob or two but I'm going to offer Vivien some money for it. I don't like to have something for nothing although I got the impression she thought we were doing her a favour by taking stuff away rather than the other way round."

Zac tapped the pocket where his wallet was tucked. "Emma said we ought to offer her something as well but like you say, I don't think she'll take anything because she said they bought the house contents for a song in the first place."

Sid turned into the main street and drove through the village. Just before the Old Bakehouse he turned into Goose Lane and tooted to Zac's father Bill who was taking something from the boot of his car. At the top of the lane he turned left towards the junction from which branched Hawthorn Road. Number thirteen was in the middle and as none of the houses had a driveway, Sid parked on the street. As he switched off the engine he glanced towards the house. "Looks like she might not be up. There's usually a light on in the living room but it's in darkness this morning."

After they stepped from the van, Zac opened the garden gate and they walked up the path. In the light from the streetlamp, Sid selected a key from the collection on his keyring.

"She's probably in the kitchen," said Zac, "I mean she does drink rather a lot of tea and coffee."

"She certainly does." Sid knocked as he unlocked the front door. Vivien had given them a key so they could come and go as they pleased and had insisted they walk straight in when they arrived in the mornings. They stepped into the hallway, closed the door and walked down the passage to the kitchen expecting to see Vivien sitting at the table eating toast and marmalade. To their surprise she was not there. Sid switched on the light. The back door was wide open. The kitchen table lay on its side, every work surface had been cleared and all appliances were piled in a corner by the fridge. Drawers were pulled from the units; cupboard doors were wide open and their contents lay scattered on the floor.

Zac moved closer to Sid. "What the devil's going on here, Sid?"

"I don't know, lad." Sid stepped back out into the hallway and from the foot of the stairs called Vivien's name. There was no answer. He felt uneasy. As he turned, he heard a cat miaow. Oscar emerged from the sitting room and sat down by the part-open door.

"Where is she, Oscar? Where's Vivien?" With caution Sid stepped over the cat. "Stay here, Zac." He pushed the door open and looked into the room.

"Oh no," he cried.

Zac instinctively ran into the room. He stopped by Sid's side.

Sprawled across the floor, on her back with a cushion next to her head was Vivien Spencer. Sid sprang forwards, kicked the cushion across to one side and fell to his knees. His hands shook as he felt for a pulse even though he knew just by looking that she was dead.

Sid stood up and took his mobile phone from his jacket pocket. "Don't touch anything, Zac. This might be a crime scene."

"A crime scene." Zac's face was white; his bottom lip trembled. He couldn't breathe. Unable to stay in the room he ran outside and sat down on the doorstep before his legs gave way.

"Oh no, this is getting to be a habit," panted Kitty, as Hetty opened the front door of Primrose Cottage to her friend on the doorstep."

Hetty gripped Kitty's arm and helped her over the threshold. "Whatever's wrong? It's not Tommy is it?"

Kitty put down her umbrella and placed it on the doormat. "No, Tommy's fine. At least I assume he is. He's not here at present because he's gone to Plymouth with Bernie. I'm not quite sure why but it's to pick up something or other for Bernie's boat."

Hetty closed the door and then guided Kitty who was shaking into the sitting room and sat her down in the armchair beside the fire. "Now sit there and compose yourself."

"Tea?" Lottie had come in from the kitchen where she had been ironing the sisters' freshly washed fancy dress costumes.

"In a minute but first both of you must sit down and hear this," Kitty's voice trembling as she spoke.

Lottie and Hetty exchanged questioning glances as they both sat down on the sofa.

"You see, in a way what I have to tell you concerns you both and that's why I've rushed round."

"It does? How?" Hetty felt uneasy.

"I've just come up from the village. As I left the post office, I saw a group of people outside the fish and chip shop talking animatedly. Not one to miss anything, I stopped to see what all the excitement was about." Kitty paused and took in a deep breath, "The person doing the telling was Pickle. You know, Percy Pickering from Hawthorn Road?" The sisters nodded, "Good, anyway, he said that Vivien thingamajig who owns number thirteen where Nigel whatsit who had a heart attack lived has been found dead on the sitting room floor."

Lottie gasped. "But that's where Zac and Sid are working."

"Exactly, that's what I meant by it concerning you both. What's more it was Zac and Sid who found her."

The colour drained from Lottie's face. "But that's terrible."

Hetty squeezed her sister's hand. "Any idea just what happened, Kitty? Was it a heart attack like Nigel?"

"I'm afraid I don't know. All Pickle was able to tell us was that at about half past eight this morning he was walking along Hawthorn Road on his way to the village to get milk from the shop and he saw several police cars and an ambulance outside number thirteen. There was no sign of anyone other than a young lad who was sitting on the doorstep despite the rain. Pickle said he asked the lad who I soon realised must be Zac, what had happened and Zac said that Vivien was dead and it looked suspicious. Before Pickle had a chance to ask anything more, a police officer came out from the house and asked Zac to go inside and not to speak to anyone for the time being. Zac did as he was told and so Pickle went straight down to the village to pass on the news as well as get some milk."

Alarmed by Kitty's revelation, Lottie rang her son, Bill, who was Zac's father. To her relief he was home and had the day off work. She repeated Kitty's news. Bill thanked her and said that he would go straight round to number thirteen to make sure Zac was alright.

In the evening, Bill drove round to Primrose Cottage to tell the sisters in person what little he knew about the death of Vivien

Spencer. Hetty insisted he sit in her favourite chair by the fire while Lottie made him a mug of tea.

"So, what can you tell us?" Hetty eagerly asked, once all were seated.

"Not a lot and needless to say, when I got to Hawthorn Road the police wouldn't let me into the house but after I explained who I was and told them I was concerned for my son's welfare, they eventually let Zac and Sid go but they were told not to leave the area."

Lottie was indignant. "Surely they don't think Zac and Sid were involved in any way with the poor woman's death."

"Who knows? But I think it's just routine and they have to keep an open mind and say that just in case."

"Yes, I suppose so."

"And I should imagine they'll both have to make statements anyway," Hetty added.

Bill nodded. "That's right especially if the results of the post mortem find that she didn't die from natural causes."

"When is the post mortem?" Lottie asked.

"Tomorrow morning."

Hetty sighed. "Sid has a good head on him. What does he make of it all?"

"He doesn't really know what to think. After we left number thirteen, we all went to Sid's place so that they could tell me what they'd seen and one thing they're both sure of is that it was a bungled robbery. The back door was wide open, you see. Someone had clearly broken in and ransacked the place because everything in the kitchen was upside-down."

"Dear, dear, whatever next," Lottie tutted, "I should imagine Zac's pretty upset."

"They both are. So now we all have our fingers crossed that the results of the post mortem will reveal natural causes."

"And when will the results be known?" Hetty asked.

"Hopefully by tea time on Thursday."

Chapter Five

Knowing that Zac had been badly shaken by the discovery of Vivien Spencer, Sid asked him if he wanted to take a couple of days off work. Zac thanked Sid but said he thought it would be better to keep working in order to take his mind off things; and so because their work at number thirteen was put on hold they opted instead to fulfil some of the smaller jobs which Sid had in his diary to do when he had the time.

On Thursday morning, the first job on the list was to mend a dripping tap at the village charity shop. Daisy and Maisie, two ladies in their sixties who ran the shop were delighted to see them. They knew it was Sid and Zac who had discovered the body of Vivien Spencer and therefore they would be the ideal pair to question although both agreed before the plumbers arrived that they must be subtle. It would most likely be a sensitive subject and for that reason they had agreed to ask no questions until they took a tea break. However, as it was the subject arose before then. For while Sid and Zac were in the back room fixing the tap, two police officers walked into the shop and asked about bags of clothing belonging to the late Nigel Taylor which they believed had been donated to the shop by his landlady Mrs Spencer. Daisy confirmed that they had two black bags containing Mr Taylor's clothes but because he was deceased neither of the ladies felt they wanted to handle the bag's contents, therefore they were untouched in the stock room. The police officers were pleased that the goods had not been tampered with and asked for the ladies to get them so they might take them away for Forensics to go through.

"Well," said Daisy, as the police officers left, "what do you think they're hoping to find in two bags of old clothes?"

Sid and Zac having heard what was said emerged from the back room. "Sounds ominous and looks like they suspect Vivien was murdered then," Sid looked grim, "It was us that told them about the bags because they wanted to know Vivien's movements on Tuesday before, well, you know."

"Terrible business," said Daisy, "She was so bright and cheery when she came in with them. It's hard to believe she's gone now."

"It is and I can understand them tracking down her last movements and so forth but what might they hope to find in the bags?" Maisie sat down on a chair behind the counter, "Damn it! I wish we'd taken a look now."

"Perhaps they're hoping to find something in one of the pockets," Daisy suggested, "You know, something that maybe the thief who broke into the house was looking for. Or maybe they're just hoping there might be a note or a letter in one of the pockets or anything that might give them some indication as to whom Nigel mixed with."

"That's interesting. So do you think the intruder was an associate of Nigel Taylor's?" Sid asked.

"Well, yes, I suppose I do but then again it's quite possible the thief was just an opportunist who having heard that Nigel was dead and the house was empty thought he'd take a look round for anything worth stealing."

"I think that's more likely to be the case," said Sid, "After all Nigel's been dead since before Christmas so surely if someone was looking for something specific he'd have tried to find it before now. Having said that, I know the Spencers asked the neighbours to switch the lights on in the evenings over the Christmas period and switch them off again in the mornings to make it look like someone was there. They closed and pulled back the curtains as well and said they'd keep an eye on the place 'til Vivien returned in the New Year. Vivien told us that on Monday during one of our many tea breaks."

"So the neighbours must have had a key," reasoned Daisy.

Sid nodded. "They did. But I know they gave it back because we were there when they dropped it in."

"Any idea who the neighbours are?" Daisy tried to recall who lived along Hawthorn Road.

"All I know is she's called Susan because Vivien said 'thanks Sue' when she brought the keys back."

"That'll most likely be the Rudds then," said Maisie, "Susan and Tim Rudd. I know they live somewhere along there."

"The Rudds. Of course, silly me. We installed an outside tap for them last year. I'm rubbish at remembering faces."

Daisy nodded. "I know who you mean. Nice couple who ran a market stall selling shoes until they retired last year. We sometimes see them in church."

The shop doorbell rang and a stranger peeped inside. "I've a bag of donations here if you'd like them."

Maisie stepped forwards to take the bag proffered. "Yes, please. Donations are always welcome."

The stranger handed over the bag, smiled sweetly, closed the shop door and left without uttering another word.

"I wonder if we'll get Nigel's old clothes back," said Daisy as she eyed the black bin liner in Maisie's hand.

Maisie shuddered. "I hope not."

"I've been meaning to take a look at this to see if it works although it seems wrong to have it now after what's happened in Hawthorn Road." Inside Primrose Cottage, Lottie wheeled the vacuum cleaner into the middle of the room and then sat down. "I do hope Zac's alright. Poor lad. Nineteen-year-olds shouldn't have to find someone dead, especially if that someone turns out to be a murder victim."

Hetty tutted. "No and nor should anyone else for that matter but let's just hope the poor woman died from natural causes."

Lottie shuddered. "It doesn't look like it though does it, Het? I mean, the place had been ransacked and Vivien wouldn't have done that. Someone must have been in there and it's highly unlikely that whoever it was, was there by invitation."

"True but it may be that she disturbed an intruder and had a heart attack when she saw the mess. Something like that." Hetty crossed her fingers.

"Let's hope so." Determined to take her mind off things, Lottie plugged the vacuum cleaner into a socket on the wall, switched it on and with little enthusiasm pushed it along the carpet by the fireplace where a few specks of sawdust lay near the wood pile. The motor sounded fine but to her dismay the cleaner did not suck anything up. She switched it off in disgust and sat down heavily on the sofa.

"Don't give up on it. I expect it just needs the bag emptying," reasoned Hetty.

"Yes, you're probably right because it seems quite heavy. Having said that, it's a different make to ours so we won't have a spare bag that fits anyway. The shape is completely different too so it's hardly worth checking."

"Don't be a defeatist, Lottie. If you take the old bag out carefully perhaps you'll be able to empty it and then reuse it until we go shopping, buy some on-line or whatever."

"Yes, that's true I suppose," she stood up, "I'll give it a go because even if it splits we can stick some tape on it and we need to test it one way or another because it's not worth spending money on new bags if it has no suction power."

Lottie pulled off the front section and looked inside. "What! Oh, for goodness sake, surely not. There's a plastic carrier bag in here, Het, and it feels chock-a-block. Men! I mean, surely Nigel didn't manage to get it to work like that."

Hetty stood up. "I can't see how he could have unless he's somehow tied it or taped it onto something or other." She chuckled, "It'd save a few pennies if it worked though."

Both sisters knelt down and Lottie gently tugged at the carrier bag. To her surprise, it wasn't connected to anything and came out with ease.

"Looks like he's simply used it as a hiding place," laughed Hetty, "Brilliant! What's inside?"

Lottie opened the bag and gasped. "It's money, Het, and loads of it." She tipped the bag's contents out onto the floor. Several bundles of twenty-pound notes bounced across the carpet.

Hetty picked up a roll. It was tightly wound and bound with an elastic band. "My goodness. How much do you reckon is here?"

"Only one way to find out."

The sisters each took a roll, removed the elastic bands and counted the notes. Both contained twenty-five.

"Twenty-five twenty-pound notes, that's five hundred pounds per roll," gasped Hetty, "I've never seen so much money."

Lottie counted the rolls; there were one hundred. "Well if every roll contains the same there is fifty thousand pounds here."

Both sisters sat staring at the money. They were speechless. After a while Hetty stood up as her legs were getting pins and needles. "What are we going to do with it, Lottie? I mean we can't keep it, can we? It must have belonged to Nigel Taylor."

Lottie looked up at her sister. "Yes it must have and I bet this is what whoever broke into number thirteen Hawthorn Road was looking for."

Chapter Six

Having driven round to Primrose Cottage following a phone call from Lottie, Debbie sat on the floor in the sisters' sitting room and looked into the empty dust bag compartment of the soon to be infamous vacuum cleaner.

"Wow! This is bonkers. So do you really think the break-in at Nigel's old house was because of the money in here?"

Hetty placed her right elbow on the arm of her chair and rested her cheek on the back of her hand. "Yes, we do Debs. It seems the perfect explanation."

"Absolutely," agreed Lottie, "and the police think so too. Het and I have discussed it and we're pretty certain now that whoever it was that broke in didn't know Vivien was staying there and he attacked her when she disturbed him. He must then have run off empty handed. Not that he could have found the money even if he hadn't been disturbed because by then it was here right under our noses not of course that we knew about it then."

"Meaning," said Hetty, "that had he broken in on Monday night instead of Tuesday he'd have got what he was looking for and we'd all be none the wiser."

Lottie tutted. "No, but sadly Vivien was there that night too so her fate might have been no different."

Debbie scrambled to her feet and sat down on the sofa beside Lottie to drink her coffee. "Any news about the post mortem yet? I mean, it is today isn't it?"

Hetty shook her head. "Yes it is and we're expecting to hear soon because if it was murder the police will contact Sid and Zac to question them further."

"And Bill's promised to ring as soon as he knows anything," Lottie prayed Vivien's death was from natural causes.

Hetty leaned forwards and thoughtfully tapped her fingers on her front teeth. "Going back to the attempted robbery. It's just occurred to me that perhaps whoever broke in didn't actually know where Nigel had the money hidden because if he did then he wouldn't have pulled out drawers and so forth, would he? I mean, it's pretty obvious that a vacuum cleaner wouldn't be kept in a drawer or under a counter cupboard."

"Maybe, or perhaps he knew where the money was kept but when he couldn't find a vacuum cleaner he assumed Nigel must have hidden it elsewhere," reasoned Lottie, "the thing is we'll never know because Nigel can't tell us and even if Vivien was still alive I should imagine she knew nothing about it at anyway. I mean, he was just her tenant and as she lived in Devon I suppose she seldom saw him as I'm sure his rent would have been paid through the bank as most things are nowadays."

"That's true but something else has just struck me," said Debbie, "I mean, how did whoever the intruder was know that Nigel had money hidden in a vacuum cleaner in the first place? It's hardly the sort of thing anyone would broadcast."

Lottie stood up and put another log into the stove. "We asked the police that but they wouldn't say or premise but we think it's possible he might have let it slip when he was in the pub. As we know drink loosens the tongue. Something like that anyway."

"I don't recall ever seeing him in the pub," Debbie finished her coffee and placed the empty mug on the floor by her feet.

"Same with us," agreed Lottie, "but then that's probably because we've no idea what he looked like and there are lots of other pubs in Cornwall anyway."

"But if he did talk while out boozing, someone could easily have overheard. People's ears are inclined to flap when money is mentioned," said Hetty, "Especially when money amounts to fifty thousand pounds. Having said that, Nigel might have been a non-drinker who had never set foot in a pub in his life."

"Maybe, but what baffles me even more is where he got the money from in the first place," said Lottie, "I mean, people usually put surplus money in the bank or invest it. I know the interest rates are rubbish at the moment but keeping it in a vacuum cleaner seems daft."

"He probably just earned it," said Debbie, "From what I've heard no-one seems to know what he did so he was probably an odd job type man or something like that who was always paid in cash."

"Ah yes, and he kept his money in the house rather than put it in the bank to avoid paying income tax," said Lottie, "That sounds feasible."

"Or he might have won it through gambling," said Hetty, "You know, poker or whatever and maybe whoever he won it from felt he'd cheated and he wanted it back."

Debbie looked around. "Where's the money now?"

"The police have it," said Lottie.

"Damn, I was going to ask if you'd let me count it. Just for the fun of it."

As they chatted the phone rang. Lottie left the room to answer it. When she returned her face was ashen.

"That was Bill," she sat down, "He's just heard from Zac that Vivien was asphyxiated. Sid and Zac have gone in to make statements."

No-one spoke until the silence was broken by a knock on the door. Hetty answered. It was Kitty who was a lot more composed than on the previous day.

"Come in," said Hetty, "Debbie's here and we've just heard from Bill that sadly Vivien was murdered."

41

Kitty's arms dropped to her sides. "Oh no, that's terrible. I'm not surprised but all the same it's still a shock."

"Would you like a coffee?" Hetty closed the door.

"Yes, please, Het. It's really miserable out there but at least it's not raining at the moment."

While Hetty went into the kitchen to make the coffee, Kitty went into the sitting room to join Lottie and Debbie. Before she sat down she warmed her hands by the fire. "Terrible news about Vivien Spencer."

"Isn't it? We're still trying to take it in." Debbie moved along on the sofa to make room for Kitty.

"I hope they don't suspect Sid and Zac," said Lottie, "after all they were probably the last people to see her alive."

Debbie looked horrified. "Oh no, I'd not thought of that. They found her too and so that may well put them in the spotlight."

Kitty sat down. "Well, it may do for a while but there won't be a motive and Zac will have an alibi assuming he was at home with Emma."

"Which he was," Lottie confirmed, "No doubt about that because Sandra said she popped in to see them when she finished work at ten on Tuesday night because they wanted her to see some of the things Zac had got from Hawthorn Road and she was there until well past eleven."

"Good," said Kitty, "At the moment I'm struggling to get my head round everything and one of the reasons I'm here is to tell you that I popped into the charity shop this morning. I wasn't intending to but as I walked by Maisie was putting some shoes in the window and she tapped on the glass and beckoned me inside. Apparently the police were at the shop this morning and took away two bags of Nigel Taylor's clothes which had been donated by Vivien Spencer."

"Ah, that would be before we told them about the money in the vacuum cleaner then," said Lottie, "They said they were trying to establish what the thieves were after."

42

"In which case it looks like the police already knew that Vivien had been murdered then," reasoned Debbie, "Either that or they suspected she had."

"Yes, makes sense. Anyway, the main reason I came round is to say that Tommy's just back from walking the dog and while out he saw Bernie who told him it's rumoured that Vivien's poor husband is here in the village now."

"Oh no. Surely not staying at number thirteen," Lottie shuddered at the thought.

Kitty shook her head. "No, apparently he's staying at the Crown and Anchor. He couldn't stay at the house if he wanted to anyway because it's still a crime scene."

"Yes, of course," Lottie felt relieved.

"That's good news then, Kitty," Hetty had heard what was said as she entered the room with Kitty's coffee.

"Good, Het?" repeated Lottie, "what's good about it?"

"Because we might see him of course. It's Friday tomorrow so I suggest we pop to the pub for a drink or two. You never know what we might find out." Hetty sat down.

"Surely you don't think the husband might be a suspect?" gasped Lottie.

"Possibly. Who knows? Remember the police always check out family members first and anyone else who's likely to benefit from a murder."

"But what motive could Vivien's husband have?" Kitty asked, "I've heard that the house is jointly owned and so are all their other properties as well."

"Precisely, but he might be a greedy so-and-so and he wants the lot. You never know there might be another woman involved. The list of motives is endless."

"But this is pure speculation, Het," said Lottie, "We don't know anything about the Spencers or their circumstances and as we agreed the other day, according to Sid she was a very nice woman and good to him and Zac for the brief time they knew her.

43

Besides, it looks as though the poor woman died because she interrupted burglars, intruders or whatever. I thought we'd already agreed that."

Hetty shook her head. "We had, but I was thinking while I made Kit's coffee that that's probably what the murderer intended it to look like. After all as far as we know nothing was taken and the fact that Vivien was a nice woman doesn't automatically mean that her husband's a nice person too."

"But nothing was taken because we think he was looking for the money in the vacuum cleaner," snapped Lottie, "which of course wasn't there."

Kitty took a sip of coffee. "Well actually it looks as though there was something taken. Tommy said it's reckoned that he, they or whatever must have pinched Nigel's laptop and mobile phone. They know he had a phone because the Spencers have his number and he must have had a laptop too because there was a charger plugged into a socket. He also had a printer but that wasn't taken."

Lottie nodded. "Yes, now you come to mention it, when Zac and Emma came round with the vacuum cleaner and books, Zac said something about Vivien not knowing what to do with Nigel's laptop and phone."

"So perhaps it wasn't the money he was after," reasoned Hetty, "perhaps it was the laptop and phone all along and so he got what he wanted."

Debbie tutted. "This is so frustrating because there's no way of finding out."

Hetty stood up to make more coffee. "Don't be negative, Debbie. We'll find out in due course. We always get there in the end but in this case it might take a little bit longer than usual."

Chapter Seven

As Hetty came indoors on Friday morning after hanging out the washing, there was a knock on the front door. Lottie was in the sitting room knitting a chunky cardigan for herself.

"I'll go, Lottie, save you getting up." Hetty dropped an old ice cream tub containing clothes pegs on the kitchen table and hurried along the hallway to the door. Outside with his arms folded against the cold wind stood a young man wearing a thin jacket; he looked no more than thirty years of age and was unknown to Hetty. Assuming he was selling something she said nothing and waited for him to speak first.

"Good morning," he peeked into the hallway, "Hmm, is this the house where the vacuum cleaner containing a lot of money now lives?"

Surprised by the question, Hetty laughed. "Yes, the vacuum cleaner does live here now. Why do you ask?"

"Oh, sorry, yes, please allow me to introduce myself. My name is Craig Western and I'm a junior journalist for one of the big tabloids." Hetty shook his offered hand. It was ice cold.

"I see. Well nice to meet you, Mr Western."

"Oh, please call me Craig."

"Alright, so what can I do for you, Craig?"

"I wondered if umm, if perhaps you'll give me an interview. Tell how you came across the vacuum cleaner and maybe even let me see it and take its picture. I'll not keep you long, I promise but I think it'll make an interesting story, don't you?"

"Hmm, maybe. Anyway, don't stand there you're letting the cold air in." Hetty, charmed by the young man's nervous chatter, opened the door wide and beckoned him to step inside.

"My sister is in there, Craig." Hetty closed the front door and pointed to the sitting room where the door was ajar, "Pop in and warm yourself up by the fire while I fetch the vacuum cleaner."

Lottie having heard the conversation on the doorstep, welcomed the surprise visitor and asked him to take a seat. She nodded to the chair nearest the fire and he gratefully sat down.

"You look frozen, young man. Did you walk up here?"

Craig was mesmerised by the speed of Lottie's clicking knitting needles. "No, no I came by car. It's not mine though. I borrowed it from a mate as mine might not have made it all the way down here. I didn't put a thick coat on because I thought it'd be nice and warm in the car but to my annoyance I couldn't get the heater to work and I'm not sure whether it's playing up or if I've been twiddling the wrong knobs."

"You must read the instructions then before you return home." Lottie spoke in a motherly way.

"Yes, I think that might be wise as it could well be bitter later especially further up the line."

"So if you work for one of the tabloids, have you driven all the way down here from London?"

"Yes."

Lottie's needles slowed. "What, just to get a story about an old Hoover?"

"Yes, we considered it worth it because…" Craig stopped mid-sentence as the door opened and Hetty wheeled in the vacuum cleaner; she stood it in the middle of the room and opened up the dust bag compartment. "This is where the carrier bag containing the money was hidden," she chuckled, "Needless to say it's no longer there or even in our possession because the police have taken it."

46

"Fascinating!" Craig left his chair and knelt down on the floor for a closer look. "May I take a few pictures?"

"Of course." Hetty left him to it and sat down on the sofa beside her sister. After excitedly taking several pictures on his mobile phone, he returned to the fireside chair. "I bet you were thrilled to bits when you found the money."

Lottie laughed. "I think we were more shocked than thrilled. I mean, it was the last thing we expected to find."

Hetty leaned forwards and rested her clasped hands on her lap. "It's only just occurred to me, Craig, but how come your paper knows about the fifty thousand pounds? I mean, it's common knowledge here, in fact we're told it's the talk of the village, but we only found it yesterday so it's not even been in the local paper yet."

"You're right, Het. So how would anyone outside Pentrillick know about it?" Lottie looked at the young journalist her eyes wide with anticipation.

Craig scratched his head. "Do you know, I've not the foggiest idea? I can only assume someone on the paper must know someone down here."

"Of course, or probably someone read about it on social media," said Lottie, "The world's a very small place these days and stories, crazes and trends spread like wildfire by the likes of Facebook and all the rest."

"Yes, I expect you're right," Hetty turned to Craig, "Anyway, are you ready to do this interview yet?"

"Yes, yes, I am," he held up his mobile phone, "Would it be alright if I recorded you talking on this? It would be so much quicker than me trying to write everything down and I don't want to miss a single word."

"Of course. Whatever suits you, Craig."

"Thank you and so when you're ready please tell me all you can starting with your names."

Lottie laid down her knitting, she and Hetty then told how the vacuum cleaner came to be in their possession and about the previous day they had made the discovery. Craig listened to their every word and asked several questions. When they concluded the story Lottie asked if he would like a cup of coffee."

"Or lunch if you're hungry," Hetty thought he needed fattening up, "It's nearly one o'clock and we usually have lunch around now."

"Oh, I don't want to put you to any trouble."

"It's no trouble. Do you like cheese on toast with a little bit of onion?"

Craig licked his lips. "I love it."

Hetty stood up. "Cheese and toast it is then."

While Hetty was in the kitchen preparing lunch, Lottie asked Craig where he lived and a little about himself. She learned that he was an only child, he shared a flat in London with three other chaps, didn't have a girlfriend and his hobby was collecting thimbles. Surprised by his hobby, Lottie went to the cupboard in the sideboard and pulled out her needlework basket. In it were two thimbles. She placed them on the palm of her hand and showed them to Craig. "Do you have ones like these in your collection?"

"Wow! No I don't have either."

"Well, if you'd like them you're more than welcome to them. I don't use thimbles and never have so they'll not be missed."

"Are you sure? They're a couple of real beauties." Craig took the thimbles from her hand and held them up to the light.

"Yes, of course. It'll make me happy knowing they're appreciated."

"In that case thank you very much."

As Lottie returned her needlework basket to the cupboard and Craig put the thimbles in his pocket, Hetty returned with three plates on a tray. She insisted their guest stayed seated by the fire and placed a plate on his lap. Craig clearly enjoyed his lunch and when his plate was empty he thanked the sisters profusely. He then rose to leave. "I think I've taken up enough of your time."

"No, you must stay a little longer," insisted Lottie, "and have a cup of tea to wash your lunch down."

"And a piece of Christmas cake," Hetty added.

"You really are too kind."

"Nonsense, it's chilly out there despite the sun and you need to keep up your intake of food and hot drinks." Lottie collected the empty plates and went to the kitchen to put on the kettle.

"So what type of stories do you cover for the newspaper?" Hetty asked.

"Crime, that's why I'm here today. My boss thought it would make a good story and chose me to get it. I was really flattered, thrilled too as I seldom get the chance to leave London."

"Well, I suppose there's enough crime up there to keep you occupied most of the time so you don't need to look elsewhere."

"Sadly that's true but I still like London."

"Yes, I can understand that, you being young. So will you be making your way back there when you leave here?"

"Sadly yes."

"Well, I hope you've enjoyed your brief stay in Cornwall, Craig, and we look forward to reading your article."

"Thank you."

After a mug of tea and a huge wedge of Christmas cake he was ready to leave; the sisters walked with him to the door. They told him to drive carefully and then waved to him until his car was out of sight.

"Do you think he really is a reporter?" Hetty asked as they returned to the sitting room.

"I did wonder, I must admit. I mean, I can't say that I've ever met a reporter before but he's certainly not what I would have expected. Especially from a national tabloid."

"Me neither but he was really sweet so let's hope he is who he claimed to be." Hetty plumped up the cushions and sat down in the chair vacated by Craig.

"Oh well, time will tell," Lottie sat down on the sofa and picked up her knitting, "If nothing appears in the newspaper over the next few days then we'll go to the police and tell them about young Craig's interest in the vacuum cleaner. Just in case they deem it suspicious. Although I'm sure that even if he isn't a reporter it'll turn out that his interest was nothing more than inquisitiveness."

"Meanwhile," chuckled Hetty, "we'll have something to tell Kitty and Debbie tonight when we go to the Crown and Anchor in search of Vivien Spencer's husband."

As Craig drove away from Primrose Cottage he remembered he needed to look at the instruction book to see how the car's heater worked and so when he reached the main street at the bottom of the hill he pulled onto the side of the road and took the booklet from the glove compartment. He soon realised that the heater worked fine and as suspected he had been twiddling the wrong knobs. With heater working, he pulled out from the side of the road to continue his journey, but as he drove through the village a thought struck him. Rather than return to London, why not stay in Cornwall for a couple of days? After all it was the weekend and it wasn't often that he found himself out in the countryside. In fact he'd never been to Cornwall before and he rather liked what he had seen so far. He left Pentrillick and when he reached the main road instead of turning right he turned left and drove in a westerly direction.

To his delight he found himself in Penzance. He liked what he saw and so booked a double room in a hotel with sea views. Eager to get work out of the way, he then wrote up his report about his interview with the sisters and emailed it to his superior who was the senior crime reporter. Satisfied with his effort he then phoned the newspaper's office and asked if he might take Monday morning off work to enable him to stay for the whole weekend. To his delight, his request was granted. He then phoned a few friends and acquaintances to tell them of his weekend break and said that he proposed to begin the drive back to London straight after breakfast on Monday morning.

As he made a cup of coffee with the facilities provided in his room he realised that he had not packed an overnight bag for he had originally planned to return home the same day. Knowing he would need a change of clothes, fresh underwear and basic toiletries, he put on his thin jacket and went for a walk through the town to buy a few items to tide him over. After he arrived back and unpacked his purchases he went downstairs to the restaurant for something to eat.

He felt conspicuous sitting alone and hoped the attractive waitress didn't assume he was on holiday and had no friends. To clarify his position as she took his order for a medium steak, chips and salad he casually dropped into the conversation that he was in Cornwall on business.

"So what line of business are you in?" she politely asked.

"I'm a journalist. My genre is crime." He spoke with pride.

"That's nice," she seemed impressed. "So are you here for a story?"

"Yes, I am and it'll be in the paper either tomorrow or Monday."

She seemed nonplussed. "But we don't get much crime down here. Not serious newsworthy stuff anyway."

"Ah, then you don't know about the fifty thousand pounds found in a vacuum cleaner."

She laughed. "Fifty thousand pounds in a vacuum cleaner! You're pulling my leg."

"I'm not. Honest."

"Hmm, right. Anyway, must get on. Would you like a drink with your meal?"

"Yes please." He ordered a pint of lager.

Tired after the drive down for which he had set off in the wee small hours, he decided to have an early night. Lexi, the waitress, had told him the forecast for the weekend was for drizzle on Saturday but dry and sunny for Sunday and so he planned to get up at a reasonable time and explore the area the following day in between bouts of drizzle. He watched the news channel on the television in his room for a while to catch up with the headlines and then climbed into bed just after nine thirty hoping not to wake before seven the following morning at the earliest.

Chapter Eight

"I think I might have spotted him," said Debbie, excitedly as she returned from the Ladies and tossed her handbag beneath the table.

"Spotted who?" Lottie's concentration was focused on the Chef's Specials' board.

Debbie sat down. "Vivien's husband of course. There are two men I've never seen before chatting outside the dining room door and I reckon one of them could be him. He's about the right age, mid-forties and he's nicely dressed so could be worth a bob or two."

"What about the chap he's with?" Hetty asked.

"He's much older. Must be well into his sixties."

"In other words, our age," Lottie laughed.

A few minutes later, the man Debbie assumed might be Vivien's husband, entered the bar and sat on one of the high stools. He was alone. The ladies watched as he spoke to Tess, who smiled, nodded, reached for a glass and then poured him a drink.

"Well, at least we know what he looks like now," said Hetty.

"That's assuming it's him," Lottie reasoned.

"True, next time I go to the bar I'll ask Tess. She's bound to know because we're told he's staying here."

As they spoke, Kitty and her husband Tommy arrived and joined the ladies at their table.

"Did you ladies see that flashy car out in the car park when you got here?" Tommy asked, "It must have cost a fortune."

The ladies all shook their heads.

Kitty sat down. "I didn't see it either until Tom pointed it out. He's always been fascinated by posh cars. Not that he'll ever have one."

Debbie nodded to towards the bar. "Must belong to the chap over there who we think is Vivien Spencer's husband. From what we hear he's worth a pretty penny."

After they had bought drinks, Tommy told an amusing story which made the ladies laugh. It put the small group in high spirits and reminded Lottie of their morning visitor. With a little prompting from Hetty she told of Craig's interest in the vacuum cleaner and that his hobby was collecting thimbles. Hetty was in the throes of adding how grateful he was to have been given lunch when the smile suddenly faded from her lips and the colour drained from her face.

Lottie clutched her sister's arm. "Are you alright, Het?" There was no response.

"Hetty, what's wrong? Are you ill?" Instinctively Lottie cast her eyes in the direction of Hetty's hypnotic gaze. She gasped. "No, it can't be. Surely not."

Debbie and Kitty looked from one sister to the other. Both appeared mesmerised by something or someone across the bar near to where the man they assumed to be Vivien's husband sat.

Hetty unsteadily stood with her hand firmly gripping the edge of the table. Across the bar, a tall, good looking, white haired man with a neatly trimmed moustache rose from his stool. His eyes and Hetty's were locked as he crossed to the table beside the fire.

"Henrietta, Henrietta Tonkins? Is it really you?"

"Charles," she whispered. Her hands were shaking.

"It is you, I can't believe it," He turned to Lottie, "and Charlotte, you're here too."

"Yes, we're both here," whispered Hetty, "We live in Cornwall now."

"Amazing. Simply amazing."

No-one noticed that Lottie was scowling.

Intrigued, Debbie smiled sweetly. "Would anyone like to introduce us?"

Debbie's voice snapped Hetty from her trance-like state. "I'm so sorry, Debbie, Kitty, Tommy, I don't know what came over me. Please allow me to introduce you to an old friend of mine, Charles Rowlett."

Charles turned to Debbie, Kitty and Tommy, he bowed his head and proffered his hand to each in turn. "Delighted to make your acquaintance, ladies, gentleman, but I must correct Henrietta because I like to think we were more than just friends."

Hetty felt the colour rise in her cheeks. "How is your wife?" she snapped.

He smiled. "If you mean Peggy, we never married."

"Oh, but I thought, I mean someone told me years ago that you were engaged."

"Yes, we were but we never married. I suppose deep down I realised that I'd made a terrible mistake. She was never the one for me despite her magnetic character." His eyes never left Hetty's face.

"You certainly did make a mistake, Charlie boy," blurted Lottie, angrily, "You damn near broke Hetty's heart when you left her for Peggy Piggy-eyes."

"Lottie, please don't." Hetty noticed the pained look in his eyes following her sister's harsh comment.

"It's alright, Henrietta. Your sister has a point and if I broke your heart, I'm sorry." He nodded courteously to the party around the table, excused himself and returned the bar where he stood beside the man who they assumed to be Vivien Spencer's husband.

55

With hands still shaking, Hetty lowered herself onto her seat and for a few moments no-one spoke. Kitty and Debbie writhed uncomfortably both po-faced for neither had ever heard Lottie speak with such vehemence. It was Tommy who broke the ice. "Would any of you ladies like another drink?" He picked up his empty glass, "because I'm having one."

All four said yes. As Tommy rose to go to the bar, Hetty rose also. "Excuse me, I need a bit of fresh air."

As she dashed out Debbie saw that tears had welled in her eyes. "Shall I go after her?"

Lottie shook her head. "No, don't. Trust me, Debbie, right now she just wants to be alone."

Kitty glanced towards the bar where Charles Rowlett had taken a seat and was chatting to the man they assumed to be Mr Spencer. "Are you alright, Lottie? I never seen you so mad."

Lottie half-smiled. "I suppose you've not and perhaps it was unjustified, but he did hurt her although she's so stubborn she'll deny it. I mean, if you ask her about her love life she'll tell you that no-one ever swept her off her feet or asked her to marry them. But that's not really true. I know for a fact that there were three chaps of whom she was very fond and one of them was Charles Rowlett. In fact he was the last and the one she cared for the most. We were all shocked when he left Het for that witch because we all thought, as did Hetty, that one day they'd get married. It was even talked about. After he went she seemed to lose interest in men and devoted herself to her work as a midwife."

Tommy arrived back with the drinks and placed them on the table. "You wouldn't be offended would you if I went and had a chat with Bernie about chaps' stuff?"

"Of course not," said Kitty, "off you go."

"Thanks," he picked up his drink and walked over towards the piano where Bernie was sitting with Sid.

"So without opening raw wounds how long ago was it that Hetty and this Charles bloke went their separate ways?" Debbie asked.

"Too many," Lottie frowned as she delved into the past. "It would have been in the mid-nineteen seventies. Yes of course, it was seventy-six. I remember that year because of the drought. Yuck, we ended up having to use standpipes back home which was awful because I had two very young children then and nappies to wash."

"That'll be forty-four years ago then come summer," calculated Kitty.

"Yes, it will."

Debbie tried to keep a straight face. "So who was this Peggy Piggy-eyes of whom you spoke with such anger? I mean surely that's not her real name."

Lottie actually smiled. "No, it's not. Her proper name is Peggy Piggott. She was actually quite nice. Pretty but in a butch sort of way and she had crooked teeth some of which overlapped. She was also knock kneed, amusing and very ambitious. She used to be a good laugh and very witty but I rapidly went off her when she stole Charles from Hetty. She had been after him for ages so we heard later from her best friend. I suppose I shouldn't blame him after all they say all's fair in love and war but I did blame him and now I've seen him again I realise that I still do."

Hetty returned to the table soon after. She picked up her drink and took a large gulp. "Before you ask, I'm alright now. It just came as a bit of a shock. I've not thought of Charles for years and certainly never expected to see him again especially in Cornwall."

All three ladies heaved sighs of relief.

"And at least we know now that Peggy didn't get him so that's made my day." Lottie looked jubilant.

"Can I just ask one thing?" Debbie glanced across the bar where the two men sat deep in conversation.

Hetty nodded. "Yes, go ahead. I'm composed now."

"Good. What I'm intrigued by is the fact that Charles spoke so formally and so precisely. I mean, you never call yourselves Henrietta and Charlotte, do you? And if you and he were romantically linked, Het, then it seems a little bizarre for him to be so formal, if you don't mind me saying so."

"You're right. Hetty and I only use our full names when dealing with something official," said Lottie, "Don't we, Het? But then Charles is a pompous ass and although his manners are impeccable there's something phoney about him."

Hetty smiled. "Lottie's right, I suppose and I've no idea why Charles is the way he is. He's always been like it though and was the same with everyone, not just us. You'll never hear him shorten a name, in fact he always referred to his parents as Mother and Father and addressed them likewise too. Which is odd because they were down to earth farmers who spoke with a rustic tongue."

"Perhaps he thinks it makes him sound superior," suggested Kitty.

"Maybe," said Hetty, "but I never asked him and I never shall."

Debbie tutted. "It's a pity he's an old flame and not an old friend because if he'd been just a friend you could get chatting to him and find out if the bloke he's with is Vivien Spencer's husband or should I say, widower."

Hetty's jaw dropped. "Of course, silly me. You're right, Debbie. I've been so wrapped up in myself that I'd momentarily forgotten that's the reason we're here tonight." She stood up, "Don't worry, I'm alright, but I'm just going to tell him there are no hard feelings and hopefully, he'll introduce us."

Kitty smiled. "I hope you're sincere with that, Het."

"I am. It was all a long time ago and it would be silly to bear a grudge." She took a large gulp of wine, "and if I'm honest, now that I've got used to the idea. It's nice to have seen him again."

Ten minutes later she returned with a smug expression on her face. She sat down. "Yes, we were spot on. He is Vivien's husband and his name is Graham Spencer. He and Charles are both staying here. Not together of course. Graham arrived yesterday and Charles this afternoon and they got chatting in the dining room over dinner this evening after having seen each other earlier on the upstairs landing. Naturally I expressed my condolences to Graham over the death of his wife. He seemed nice anyway. His voice is gentle and there is definitely sadness in his eyes."

"Not the sort to murder his wife then?" Debbie asked.

"Good heavens no. Graham Spencer is no murderer."

"Which reminds me," said Kitty, "Do we know exactly how the poor lady died yet?"

Hetty looked aghast. "Good heavens, we are slipping, aren't we? We know she was asphyxiated but that's all. Drink up ladies then I can ask Tess."

"Did someone call my name?"

All looked up. Tess was collecting empty glasses.

Hetty looked sheepish.

Tess knew the ladies well. "So what did you want to know?"

"Hmm," Hetty looked around to make sure they were not overheard, "How poor Vivien died," she whispered. "We know the cause of death but not what happened."

"Well, we did think of popping round to see Zac to get the latest, didn't we, Het?" Lottie reminded her sister, "but we decided against it as it wouldn't be fair to make the poor lad relive finding her again."

"Yes, of course, that's right, we did."

"So do you know exactly what happened, Tess?" Debbie asked.

Tess nodded and leaned over their table. "Well, I've heard from a very good source, namely Sidney Moore, that she was knocked onto the floor and suffocated with a loose cushion from the three piece suite."

Chapter Nine

On Saturday morning, Pentrillick held its first indoor market in the village hall. It was a joint venture organised by producers of local food, arts, and crafts to enable themselves and stall holders who'd had pitches at the annual Christmas Wonderland at Pentrillick House to have somewhere to sell their wares all the year round.

Hetty and Lottie, keen to see who was there and to support the new venture left Primrose Cottage just after ten in the morning and walked down Long Lane, umbrellas up, with an air of anticipation.

To their delight they found the village hall busy with a buzz as people happily snapped up bargains, especially vegetables, dairy produce and daffodils from the stall run by the Glovers a farming family who ran an efficient business a mile or so outside the village.

Other stalls sold hand knitted garments and toys, small hand crafted wooden wheelbarrows for displaying plants, handmade jewellery, pottery, cakes, plants, handmade candles, soap and vintage clothes. By a stall selling wooden house name plates, Norman was looking at different designs. "Ah, two ladies of good taste. I want to have a name plate made for 'Wits' End'. Which do you think is the most attractive?"

After looking through the numerous designs, Hetty and Lottie both agreed that Norman's favourite would be their choice too.

After leaving Norman to place his order, the sisters bought a dozen free range eggs and two saffron buns. They toyed with the idea of a wheelbarrow to enhance their front garden for the Pentrillick in Bloom competition later in the year but decided to leave it until another week when they would take the car to transport it. On the vintage clothes stall, Hetty bought a midi-length dress simply because she had owned an identical one when in her early twenties.

"I know it's silly," she said to her sister as they made their way home, "but I always loved that dress and so I've bought it for old time's sake."

"I don't think it's silly at all. It's nice to look back on old memories and let's face it, Het, when you get to be our age there are a lot to look back on." Lottie wanted to ask Hetty if she genuinely regretted never having married. It was a subject that had arisen many times over the years and Hetty always said she was happy with the way her life had panned out. But Lottie having seen her sister's reaction to the unexpected re-emergence of Charles Rowlett wondered if Hetty was being truthful. Sadly she acknowledged it was a question to which she would never receive an honest answer. "So do you think you'll ever wear the dress?"

"Probably but not before the summer of course and then it would have to be for Sunday best as it's too nice for everyday wear. It should fit me anyway because it's a bigger size than my original."

"My size and weight has changed very little over the years," teased Lottie, "In fact if anything I'm probably a bit smaller than I used to be."

"Humph, alright for some." Hetty had to work very hard to keep off the pounds which she thought was very unfair.

Zac and Emma planned to spend much of the Saturday at the Old Bakehouse with Zac's family. Sandra, Zac's mother, had invited them having heard from Emma that he was depressed following the discovery of Vivien Spencer. It was hoped the visit would have a therapeutic effect and help restore Zac to his old self.

As Zac and Emma locked up their house on the new estate in the afternoon, they saw Polly Digsby walking towards them with Barnaby on his lead.

"Hello gorgeous," Emma crouched down and petted the little Scottie dog, "It's not very often we see doggies like you these days which is silly because you're a beautiful boy."

Polly removed the dog's lead. "You're right and that's because Scotties are a dying breed. I read about it somewhere a while back and when I told Jay he went off to the rescue place to see if he could find one for me and he found Barnaby. When he brought him back and I saw him it was love at first sight."

"He's very friendly," said Zac.

"He is now but we reckon he'd been badly treated because when we first got him he didn't like people and now it's the other way round and he doesn't like being left on his own."

"We often talked of getting a dog," said Zac, "but with both of us working it wouldn't be practical so it'll have to wait for a few years."

"Well that's where we're lucky. With me working a few days on and a few days off and Jay working from home there's always someone around to keep this mutt company and if Jay wants to go out while I'm away, he takes Barnaby with him."

"Like to the pub," laughed Emma.

"Oh yes, they're both very fond of the pub and who can blame them. The Crown and Anchor is the nicest pub I've ever known and James and Ella are smashing."

After Polly and Barnaby had continued their walk through the estate to their home, Rainbow's End, Zac and Emma set off in the opposite direction arm in arm. Once out of the estate they turned right and walked down the narrow lane into the main street towards the Old Bakehouse which lay at the far end of the village.

They were greeted warmly by Bill, and Sandra who promptly put on the kettle and produced a cherry cake which she knew to be Zac's favourite. "I have to confess that I didn't make the cake," said Sandra, "I bought it from the indoor market this morning so I'm not sure who concocted it."

The family spent the afternoon chatting about this and that, all careful to avoid the subject of the village's latest murder.

At half past six, Zac's younger twin sisters, Vicki and Kate, changed their clothes ready for work at the Crown and Anchor where they had part time jobs waitressing which fitted in with their school A-level work.

"I don't expect we'll be late," said Vicki, "I should imagine it'll be quietish now Christmas is over and done with."

"And you won't want to linger now that young Harry's gone back to uni," teased Bill.

Kate's shoulders slumped. "Hmm, it's not the same when he's not there. Still, soon be Easter and then he'll be back again."

"Don't wish your lives away," said Sandra, "time goes quite quickly enough as it is. Although I must admit, day after day of constant rain is making this winter drag somewhat."

"You can say that again," said Emma, "some areas of the grounds at Pentrillick House are waterlogged and have been for several weeks."

"Never mind," said Bill, as the girls left the house, "soon be summer. Meanwhile I suggest the best way we while away this particular winter's evening is to play Monopoly."

Sandra groaned. "Oh, Bill, we've not played that for years."

"Exactly, and I think it's time we did. I'm feeling lucky tonight."

"Well, I'm game," said Emma, "as long as I can have the little dog who reminds me of Barnaby."

64

"Yeah, why not," agreed Zac, "Could be a laugh."

Bill stood up. "We'll need to have a drink with it, so I'll deal with that while you find the game, Sandra."

Rather than go in the dining room they stayed in the living room and sat around the small table in the corner so they could benefit from the log burner's heat. Bill opened a bottle of wine for the ladies; he and Zac had cans of lager.

As he had hoped, Bill won easily, leaving the other three with very little money.

"It's not fair, I never win at anything." Sandra's face was sulky.

"Yes, you do, Mum. Remember you used to do competitions and won quite a few things here and there." Zac, having consumed a few drinks and enjoyed plenty of laughter was in a much happier frame of mind.

"A few things here and there!" gasped Bill, "If you remember it was your mother winning a three-week holiday at Sea View Cottage that caused us all to get to know Pentrillick in the first place. Were it not for that, we wouldn't be living here now."

Emma took Zac's hand, "And we would never have met."

Sandra's face lit up. "Yes, I'd sort of forgotten that's how it all happened. What a lot of water has passed under the bridge since then."

Inside the Crown and Anchor, recently widowed Graham Spencer sat by the fire talking to Charles Rowlett. Both men, on their own and having lodgings at the pub, had struck up a friendship and were enjoying a drink after having eaten in the dining room.

"So what line of business were you in before your retirement?" Graham asked.

"I was a dentist and worked for a practice in Kensington."

"Really! I don't think I'd like looking in people's mouths all day long."

"A lot of people say that but like most things, you get used to it."

"So are you still living in Kensington or did you move out into the countryside after you retired?"

"I'm still there because I love it, so I must be a city boy at heart even though I was born and bred in the countryside." Charles, warmed by the fire, unbuttoned his tweed jacket, "How about you, Graham? Where do you live, work and so forth?"

"I live in Devon and property development's my bent. I started out as a brickie and then inherited a few grand from an aunt. With that I bought a rundown house, did it up and sold it for a profit. A couple of years later I married Vivien who was a hairdresser. We bought another place with the proceeds from the last sale and did the same. Eventually we had a fair bit of money behind so Vivien gave up work and we started to rent out the properties rather than sell them. Viv looked after the furnishing side of things and I did the maintenance and now we have thirty-eight would you believe?"

"Gosh, that must bring in a tidy sum then."

"It does but there's a fair bit of maintenance work involved. You know, someone needs the heating fixed or a fence has blown down. I use those examples because they were the latest incidents. The last place we actually bought was the one here in Hawthorn Road. That was two years ago and Nigel was our first and last tenant there. Our long-term plan was, as we got older, to offer all tenants who'd been in residence for ten years or more the chance to buy them at a favourable price. That was Vivien's dream anyway and I shall make sure her wishes are upheld in her memory. In fact I shall probably sell off half of them this year and put some of the money to good causes."

"Sounds like she was a virtuous woman."

"She was. She was one of the best and it'll be hard to manage without her."

"I admire you for your stoicism."

"Thank you, I'm doing it for Viv. She said one of the things she liked about me was my ability to stay strong and so I can't let her down." Graham cast his eyes around the bar, "It's daft I know but I feel that she's still with me, watching, you know, to make sure that I can cope."

"Any children?"

"Two, both grown up. One's at university and the other has just got married and lives in Coventry now."

"So they're not near you?"

"No, but I have very good neighbours and friends too."

"Phew, it's warm in here." Charles took a crisp white handkerchief from his pocket and wiped his brow. "I might have to remove my jacket or sit further away from the fire."

"Here swap seats. It's cooler on this side of the table."

After changing places, Graham, keen to change the subject, pointed to a notice pinned on the wall beside the French doors. "I've only just seen that. Are you any good at quizzes?"

Charles laughed. "Depends what the questions are. I'm pretty good at general knowledge but hopeless when it comes to sport. I don't watch a great deal of television either and wouldn't know one soap from another so could come unstuck there and don't think many quizzes include questions about dentistry."

"We might be able to make a bit of a team then. I'm fanatical about sport and Viv and I have several favourite television programmes that we don't like to miss," he sighed deeply, "Don't think I'll be able to watch them now she's gone though. Be too painful."

"Without being indelicate, have the police any idea who took your wife's life?"

"No, I don't think so. I mean, they're pretty sure she must have disturbed a burglar but who he was they've no idea but no doubt the bastards thought there was no-one in the house. Poor Viv. If only she'd stayed here instead. I said she ought to because having the bathroom done meant she'd be without a shower and a loo for a while but she wouldn't hear of it. She said there was a separate downstairs loo so that was no problem and it wouldn't hurt to make do with a wash for a couple of days. I wish I'd put my foot down now."

"Oh dear, but you mustn't blame yourself."

"I try not to but it's hard."

"So was anything taken from the house?"

"It's not really possible for me to say. I mean, I wasn't that familiar with its contents but it looks like Nigel's phone and laptop have gone because the chaps doing the new bathroom told the police they were both there when they finished work on the day Viv died. They remember it well because Viv said she wasn't sure what to do with them."

Charles frowned. "Who is Nigel?"

"Nigel, Nigel Taylor, he was the last tenant. The one who died of a heart attack just before Christmas."

"Ah, yes, of course. I remember you saying about him now. Poor chap. Any idea how old he was?"

"Fifty-three."

"Good heavens. That's no age."

"No it isn't," Graham stood up. "Anyway, another scotch? I'm having one, it'll help me sleep."

Charles stood also and quickly drained his tumbler. "Yes, but let me get them."

"No, you sit down. You got the last ones, it's my turn now."

68

Chapter Ten

Sunday morning dawned bright and sunny and so after breakfast, Hetty and Lottie walked down Long Lane and into the village for Sung Eucharist in the church. It was the second Sunday in Epiphany and to Hetty's delight the service began with one of her favourite hymns 'Brightest and Best are the Sons of the Morning'. It had been a favourite since 1974 when she as a young twenty-two-year-old had first met Charles Rowlett at a New Year's Eve party the previous Monday. As Hetty sang her mind drifted back. New Year's Day in 1974 was the first to be a public holiday and so people celebrated more freely than in previous years. She recalled the moment she was introduced to Charles; her knees had weakened. She really did think he was the brightest and best.

When the hymn finished and the congregation sat down, Hetty felt her sister's elbow nudge her arm. "Why are you grinning, Het?" Lottie hissed.

"Am I?"

"Yes, like a Cheshire cat. Vicar Sam noticed and I saw him smile."

Hetty placed her hand over her mouth. Her cheeks reddened. "I'll tell you later." But as the words left her lips she realised Lottie might not share her enthusiasm for the trip down memory lane and so she spent the rest of the service trying to think of a plausible fabricated reason to fob off her sister should she remember to ask.

On Sunday evening the sisters walked down Long Lane with Kitty. Their destination the Crown and Anchor for the first quiz night.

Inside they found Debbie already waiting, a glass of wine in her hand. "I tried to get Gideon to come since he's quite clever but he wouldn't. More's the shame."

Kitty sat down. "I tried to do the same with Tommy. He's not particularly clever but he does know rather a lot of obscure facts."

"Is there a limit as to how many are allowed in a team?" Lottie saw that there were six people around the table by the piano.

"No more than half a dozen," said Debbie, "I asked Ella when I bought my drink."

Hetty cast her eyes around the bar. "We could do with a couple more then."

"Perhaps your Charles will be in," said Debbie, impishly, "then we can nab him."

"He's not my Charles and he's here already." Hetty nodded towards a table on the opposite side of the bar where Charles sat with Bernie and wife Veronica, Sid the plumber, and Graham Spencer.

"Humph, he's not wasting his time making friends," scoffed Lottie.

Hetty sprang to his defence. "Maybe he was on his own and they asked him to join them. All on that table are very affable."

"Most likely," Debbie agreed, "and we know that he and Graham get on as both are staying here, and no doubt, Sid, Bernie and Veronica are trying to get Graham involved to help take his mind off his wife's awful murder for a while."

"And I am sure Charles will be doing the same," said Hetty generously.

As Kitty was about to speak the front door of the pub opened and in walked Lottie's son Bill and Sandra his wife.

"Problem solved," Lottie stood up and beckoned the late arrivals over to join them.

"Ideal," Bill unzipped his jacket, "because we'd be pretty useless if it were just the two of us."

"Useless!" shrieked Sandra, "Speak for yourself, William Burton."

"I'll go and get us a drink," chuckled Bill, "Are you ladies ready for another yet?"

"I'm fine thanks," said Kitty. Hetty and Debbie agreed.

"We don't want to drink too much before the quiz," reasoned Lottie, "as it might dull our memories."

When Bill returned with a pint for himself and a white wine for Sandra he sat down with the ladies.

"So what are your best subjects, Bill?" Debbie asked.

"Umm, well, I know a bit about gardening, woodwork and marketing food. Oh yes, and I'm pretty knowledgeable about country music too."

"Marketing food," spluttered Sandra, "I believe we're doomed, ladies."

"But I do know lots about marketing food. It's what I do at work."

"Hmm, maybe but I can't see it being of any use tonight."

"Country music might though," Kitty felt she ought to be generous.

Before the quiz began, James asked everyone to either turn off their phones or at least promise not to use them. Sid suggested everyone place their phones in the middle of their tables to make sure that no-one cheated. Everyone appeared to agree and so all did as Sid suggested. James then read out the questions and team leaders wrote down the answers on sheets of paper provided. Halfway through they took a fifteen minute break for refilling glasses and trips to the loo. After the last question was asked at the end of the quiz, the papers were collected for marking and raffle tickets were sold in aid of the

Christmas lights fund. The raffle was drawn after the quiz results were announced. Lottie, Hetty and their team were not amongst the top three winners but Bill did win a prize in the raffle; an Indian curry recipe book.

"Ideal. Just what I need as I've often looked at the spices at work and thought I really must get into curries because I enjoy eating them." Bill worked for one of the large supermarket chains.

"Well, I hope you do," said Sandra, "It would be really useful if you did the cooking occasionally and a nice curry on a winter's night would be very welcome."

Bill flicked through the pages and then closed the book. "I shall take it with me to work tomorrow and look through it in my lunch break. Then before I leave I'll get the necessary ingredients and cook you whatever I've chosen to do."

"Perfect," because I'm doing the night shift tomorrow so will need something before I go."

Sandra worked as a carer at the care home for the elderly in the village which was in the lane just below the new housing estate, Cobblestone Close.

"Talking of curries, has anyone seen that?" Debbie pointed to a notice above the bar stating - *Curry nights coming soon. Details to be announced later.*

"Ideal," chuckled Bill, "that'll spur me on even more."

A little later, Hetty went to the bar for drinks and as she waited Charles appeared by her side.

"May I get your drinks, Henrietta?"

"Oh no, I wouldn't dream of it, Charles. There are six of us and so that would be very grossly unfair."

"Perhaps another time then."

"Maybe." Were Hetty's hands not visible resting on the bar she would have crossed her fingers. Not that Charles would have noticed for his eyes were focused on her face. "So to use an old hackneyed saying, do you come here often?"

Hetty laughed. "Too often some might say. Apart from tonight for the quiz, we're always in on Tuesdays after we've been to bingo in the village hall. We often pop in after drama group meetings too but I don't think any of us are going to be in this year's play and if that's the case we'll not be going to any of the rehearsals. We'll find out on Wednesday anyway as that'll be the first of this year's meetings. And then there's the Gardening Club on Mondays but we're taking a break during January. And then of course we sometimes pop in on Fridays or other nights for that matter if there's something on."

"Good heavens. Never a dull moment in village life then."

"No, no there's not and I love it here."

Ella approached Hetty and took her order. At the same time Tess asked Charles what he'd like.

"So what brings you to Cornwall, Charles?" Hetty asked as their drinks were poured.

"Poldark. I saw the scenery and thought I really ought to take a trip down west some time. I'd never been here before, you see."

Hetty frowned. "But Poldark hasn't been on the television since last summer."

"I know and that's why I didn't come down then. I thought being summer it'd be too busy. After that I forgot all about it but was reminded the other day when I saw a copy of Winston Graham's book *The Twisted Sword* in the library. So when I got home I Googled Cornwall and read a little of its history and then as I had nothing on for a while, I chucked a few things in my car and here I am. I must say I rather like the place in the winter and I was mesmerised watching the sea from the window in my room here the other day."

"I agree, Cornwall is lovely whatever the season although I think we get more than our fair share of rain."

"I had noticed, not that I mind the rain. Unless I have to go out, that is"

Hetty took her purse from her handbag. "So what made you come to Pentrillick, Charles?"

"Ah, well for some reason I thought I'd head towards Penzance because if you remember I was a great enthusiast for Gilbert and Sullivan's works and especially the *Pirates of Penzance* in which I played a leading part one year with our local operatic society. But as I was driving along the main road I saw a turning for Pentrillick and something made me slow down and drive through the village. When I saw the pub and realised it did accommodation I stopped, came in and here I am." He gazed into Hetty's eyes, "Perhaps it was fate."

Hetty felt uncomfortable. "Hmm, maybe. So how long are you here for?"

Charles shrugged his shoulder. "I don't know. Until I get fed up, I suppose. I'm retired now so there's nothing to rush back for. My time's my own and James tells me my room will not be required until half term towards the end of next month."

Ella placed a tray on the bar on which were Hetty's drinks. Hetty paid with her bank debit card and then picked up the tray. "Anyway, it's good to see you again, Charles and I hope you enjoy your stay here."

"I'm sure I shall especially if we get the chance to chat again some time."

Hetty smiled sweetly and returned to her family and friends.

Inside the room of his Penzance hotel, junior crime reporter Craig Western took a shower, put on the new shirt he had bought in the town and left his room to go out for the evening. As he passed the hotel restaurant he saw Lexi and waved. She waved back. He smiled; it was good to see a friendly face.

After he left the hotel by the main entrance he walked along the promenade and then stopped, rested his hands on the railings and looked down onto the beach. The tide was in and he stood for a while enjoying the sound of the sea and watching the rolling waves as they splashed onto the shore in the light of a full moon. Craig was mesmerised. Having lived inland for the duration of his life he had spent very little time by the sea; just the occasional holidays most of which were taken abroad where the sea was calm, blue and predictable. When his hands grew cold he tucked them inside his pockets and then continued on his way tunefully whistling the theme tune from his favourite television show. The weekend had flown by and he had really enjoyed his impromptu stay. On Saturday afternoon he had dodged the showers and browsed every charity shop in the town where he found three unusual thimbles to add to his collection. On Sunday, because the weather was fine and sunny he had caught the train to St. Ives, wandered around the popular tourist destination and then returned to his hotel before dark. Delighted with the way things had panned out and sorry that he had to go home the following day he had decided that for his last night he would go to the same pub that he had visited the previous evening. There he planned to have a few pints and then afterwards to get a takeaway on his way back to the hotel.

Inside the Nag's Head, Craig bought a pint of real ale brewed in Cornwall and then sat down near to the fire glad of the warmth. Several people were in and he soon realised why; Sunday night, as in Pentrillick, was quiz night. Craig wished that he was not alone for he liked quizzes and had a good head for general knowledge. As he stood to get another drink, a man also alone asked if he'd like to join him and make a small team. Craig readily accepted and the man introduced himself as Don Pascoe.

After the quiz, Craig said goodbye to Don and thanked him for his hospitality. He regretted having to leave, especially as the landlord had put on a CD of songs by a Cornish male voice . choir, but he had a long drive ahead of him the next day and so needed to get a good night's rest. Don, pleased to have had company, wished Craig a good trip home and hoped he'd enjoyed his brief stay.

Craig left the Nag's Head at ten o'clock and strolled along the road singing the tune he'd heard the male voice choir singing as he'd left the pub. Slightly light-headed after the strong beer, he headed towards the town, happy to have had an enjoyable evening. With a spring in his step and a grin on his face, he passed by a barber's shop and he laughed out loud when he saw his reflection in the window. At the same time, his stomach rumbled; realising he was hungry, he pulled his phone from his pocket to establish where he might purchase a takeaway. As he neared the end of the road he heard a car engine start up alongside him. Without giving it a second glance he continued on his way. At the junction he looked in all directions, the dark coloured vehicle he had heard was stationary, its engine ticked over and its lights were dimmed. Other than cars parked alongside the kerb, no other vehicles were around and so he stepped off the pavement to cross the road. The headlights of the stationary vehicle suddenly blazed on full beam. Craig, momentarily dazzled, squinted and raised his arm to shield his eyes. The car's engine revved noisily and its tyres screeched. Alarmed by its speed as it leapt towards him, Craig stumbled backwards and cursed as his phone flew from his hand. A loud thud on impact was followed by a scream and Craig's body was knocked flying into the air. As he landed a motionless crumpled heap in the middle of the road, the vehicle sped off down a one-way street and out of sight.

Chapter Eleven

"Oh no, I don't believe it," screamed Lottie.

It was almost half past eight on Monday morning and Hetty was in the kitchen making mugs of tea when she heard her sister's cry. With mugs in hand she dashed into the sitting room where Lottie had switched on the television; the local news was on. Lottie pointed to the screen where police cars were parked in a Penzance street.

"It's Craig Western," said Lottie, "he's been knocked down and is in a bad way."

"What!" Hetty handed Lottie a mug of tea and then sat down beside her on the sofa. Neither spoke as they listened to the reporter near to the police tape asking for witnesses or anyone who knew who Craig Western was. His phone had been crushed in the collision but a bank card found in his pocket enabled him to be identified. The police were keeping an open mind as to whether it was deliberate or an accident. But either way, the driver of the vehicle had not stopped and reported the incident and as no-one was around when it happened there were no witnesses. Mr Western was in Treliske hospital with life threatening injuries. The incident happened between ten and eleven on Sunday evening and he was found shortly after by a Wesley Street resident who was on his way home from a restaurant where he worked.

"If it was deliberate why on earth would someone want to harm him?" Hetty switched off the television to enable her to think clearly, "He was a smashing bloke."

"He was and I expect it was an accident. I mean, the person responsible had probably been drinking and was way over the limit."

"Most likely or even high on drugs."

"True, but as regards Craig, I wonder why he was in Penzance. He came to see us on Friday morning so I would have thought he'd have long since gone home."

"Perhaps he fancied a break and decided to stay a little longer."

Lottie's hands were shaking. "But if his being run down was deliberate, do you think we ought to tell the police that he was here the other day, Het? After all the fact he was asking about the vacuum cleaner and its contents might mean there's a connection somewhere between him, Vivien Spencer and the house in Hawthorn Road."

"Hmm, I'm not sure. Let's leave it for a while because if he's been in the area all weekend, he must be staying somewhere local so when that hotel or whatever hears of the accident then they'll no doubt come forward and contact the police. They'll also be able to give them his home address and so forth. After all we don't know anything about him other than the fact he's a junior reporter who lives in London and collects thimbles."

"That's a good point and of course it might not be the same Craig Western anyway." Lottie's hopes rose.

"I hadn't even thought of that so let's hope you're right but sadly I've a feeling that won't be the case."

Shortly after there was a knock on the door. It was Debbie. "I've just heard the news about the reporter chappie. That's if he really is a reporter, it didn't say, did it? But then that's probably because they don't know anything about him other than his name."

After Debbie stepped inside, Lottie closed the door quickly to keep out the strengthening wind. "You've answered you own question, Debbie, but we know what you mean."

"Well, when I heard on the local radio station this morning I didn't think anything of it although at the back of my mind I felt the name rang a bell. It didn't come to me until about ten minutes ago when I realised that he must be the chap who came to interview you about the vacuum cleaner." Debbie unzipped her coat and hung it on the newel post at the foot of the stairs.

"Yes, although of course having spent some time with him we recognised the name instantly. We're both quite upset by it because he seemed ever so nice. Although Hetty was a bit worried by the fact he asked if we'd had anything else from the house in Hawthorn Road."

"And he kept glancing around the room even when he was talking," Hetty called from the sitting room.

"Did he? You didn't mention that the other day. How weird. I wonder what else he thought you might have." Debbie caught sight of her windswept hair in the hall mirror and attempted to straighten it.

"No idea, but at the moment we have our fingers crossed that it's a different Craig Western anyway."

"Oh, I never thought of that but I suppose it could be as neither Craig nor Western are unusual names."

Lottie led Debbie into the sitting room where Hetty sat beside the fire with Albert her Yorkshire terrier on her lap.

"I heard what you've been saying but as you can see I can't get up."

Debbie stroked Albert's head and then sat down. "Are you alright, Het? You look a bit pale."

"Yes, I'm fine. Just a little sad. I mean one person has died, another is unconscious and it seems the vacuum cleaner is the cause. Not directly of course but it's almost as though it's cursed."

Debbie bit her lip to stop herself from smiling. The idea of a cursed vacuum cleaner seemed a ludicrous proposition.

Hetty and Lottie insisted Debbie stay for lunch which she was happy to do as her husband, Gideon was at work where he had a part-time job as a gardener at Pentrillick House. While they ate Lottie switched on the television for the local news to see if there were any updates. There were. Police confirmed that Craig Western was a journalist who lived in London and was staying at a Penzance hotel for the weekend. It was also known that he had been in the Nag's Head public house prior to the accident and the police were keen to hear from anyone who had been in the pub that evening and spoken to him. They were also keen to speak to anyone who knew why he was in Cornwall as a waitress at the hotel had informed them that he was in Cornwall on business.

"We better give the police a ring then," said Lottie as she switched off the television, "as it seems we might have a piece or two of useful information."

On Wednesday evening, the sisters went to a meeting for the Pentrillick Players where details of the group's latest production were to be discussed with Robert Stephens who produced and directed the group's plays. The meeting went well and as usual Robert said that copies of the script would soon be available at the post office for anyone wishing to audition for a part. After the meeting, Lottie, Hetty, Debbie and Kitty went to the Crown and Anchor to mull over the play's plot.

"Will you be after a part this year, Het?" Debbie asked as they sat at their favourite table beside the fire.

Hetty shook her head. "No, the recent murder of poor Vivien Spencer and the apparent hit and run involving Craig Western has rather taken the wind out of my sails and I'd much

80

sooner focus on trying to fathom out who was responsible for those cases than learn lines. Besides, there are a lot of people in the group now so they don't need me and it's nice to help with the backstage stuff."

"In which case none of us here will be treading the boards this year," said Kitty, "Not that I ever have as you all well know."

"Same here," said Lottie, "my talents go no further than helping with the costumes."

"So is there any more news as regards Craig?" Kitty asked.

Hetty shook her head. "No, the police called to see us after we rang them but by then they already knew about Craig's vacuum cleaner story because they had found his laptop under the bed in his hotel room and so put had two and two together. As for his condition, we've no idea and it's no good ringing the hospital because they won't tell us as we're not related."

"But to be fair, Het, the police told us they believed there was no change."

"And when there is an improvement they'll probably move him nearer home," said Debbie, "You know, back to London."

"If there ever is an improvement," sighed Hetty.

"I'm sure there will be and at least we know now that he was a genuine reporter," said Lottie, "I thoroughly enjoyed his little article in the paper and he managed to put an amusing twist to it."

"I thought the same," agreed Debbie, "and for that reason I've already put the newspaper in my ottoman full of keepsakes."

Hetty nodded her head towards two young men who had just taken seats on the high bar stools. "Forgive me for changing the subject but does anyone know who they are?"

"They're daffodil pickers," Kitty waved when she caught their eyes; they waved back. "Don't you remember them? They've been here since the beginning of the month and were here this time last year too and for several years before that as well but I couldn't say how many. They'll stay for as long as the daffodils need picking and then go off somewhere else to harvest other crops and so forth."

"Oh, I must have seen them before then but I don't remember," Hetty admitted, "but then we do see a lot of people in here over a year."

"Well, I must admit it's the first time I've seen them this season but Tommy told me they were here because he was chatting to them recently. For some reason the lads get on well with Tommy. Probably because he's a countryman and so they have something in common."

"So are they foreigners?" Debbie asked.

Kitty shook her head. "No, they're not. I don't know where they're from but they're definitely natives who live in a motorhome and like the freedom of travelling around."

"Good for them," said Lottie, "but it wouldn't suit me. I like the comforts of a home too much not to mention the security of bricks and mortar."

Debbie drained her glass. "So which farm will they be working at?"

"Willow Farm, you know the Glovers' place," said Kitty, "that's the only farm around here that grows daffodils."

"Of course. That was a silly question."

"Jimmy Glover's very good to them," Kitty continued, "He lets them park their home in the farmyard and insists they use the bathroom in the house. He even leaves the door unlocked for them and Tamsin, his wife, frequently bakes them a pasty each for when they get back in the evening."

After two pints of beer the young men rose from the barstools and headed for the door but on the way out they greeted Kitty.

"Off already?" she said.

"Yep, got an early start. Well, as early as the daylight permits this time of year."

Kitty introduced the men to her friends as Gus and Tony. All shook hands.

"I should imagine it's back breaking work picking daffodils," said Lottie, "even for young men like you."

"It is," agreed Gus, "but you get used to it. Our favourite crop is strawberries though. The farm we go to grows them under cover and up from the ground so not too much bending. A real contrast to the daffs."

"Yeah, it's a right doddle in comparison," said Tony. "Although being summer it can get a bit warm in the polytunnels."

Gus pulled up the hood of his jacket. "Be a few months yet 'til strawberry time though and right now, when our fingers get frozen, it's hard to imagine getting hot in the sweltering heat."

Debbie licked her lips. "Hmm, strawberries and cream, blue skies, hot sunny days, cricket and Wimbledon…bliss."

Chapter Twelve

"What's that you're reading?" Lottie found Hetty curled up in a chair beside the fire when she returned from the village shop with a container of milk and a packet of chocolate digestive biscuits.

"It's one of the books from number thirteen. It was written before we were born and I've never heard of the author but the first few pages seem quite good," Hetty closed the book and placed it on the arm of her chair. "By the way, I've taken the rest of the books out of the box now and they're on the shelf in the alcove by the fireplace because I should imagine after what happened at number thirteen we're hardly likely to get the bookcase from there now, which is a shame."

"I very much doubt if we will either. Still never mind and you've saved me a job with the books as I've been meaning to empty that box for some time but as we never have the radiator on in the dining room it's always too cold. So what have you done with the ornaments that were on the shelf?" Lottie removed her shoes and put on her slippers which she had left warming by the fire.

"They're on top of the piano. It looks a bit cluttered but it'll do for now."

"Well done. Anyway, tea?"

Hetty chuckled. "Need you ask?"

As Lottie switched on the kettle, Kitty knocked on the door. Hetty let her in.

"I've just been to see Betsy Triggs and she told me something that might be of interest."

"Really." Hetty closed the door and called to Lottie in the kitchen. "Make an extra cup, Lottie. Kitty's here."

"Will do."

Hetty led Kitty into the sitting room.

"Hmm, those hyacinths smell gorgeous. Their scent fills the room. I'll make sure I grow some next Christmas."

"It's well worth it and is something Lottie and I have always done as did our dear old mum when we were kids. They're not always out in time for Christmas but I think we appreciate them more in January especially when the weather's grotty."

Kitty sat down. "Not been too bad these past few days though, has it? And it's lovely out today now the frost has cleared. I don't mind frost as it's very pretty and better than snow and now the sun's out I'll probably do a bit of weeding this afternoon although I daresay I'll talk myself out of it."

"Funny you should say that because when I hung the washing out this morning I contemplated doing the same. I pulled up a few bits of hairy bittercress on my way back indoors but the ground struck so cold and damp that I decided against it," Hetty sat down in her usual chair by the fire.

"I suppose you're right. I think I'll go for a long walk instead."

"So what's Betsy's news?" Hetty asked.

"Well, she seemed a bit nervous which is unusual for Betsy as she's pretty bombproof but apparently she's been hearing noises coming from Sea View Cottage and last night she saw two blokes go in there. She wondered if I knew who they were because she's heard nothing about anyone moving in and the place has been empty since Ivor and Sophie moved up to Cobblestone Close. I did think I'd ring Brett and see if he's got new tenants but I didn't want to bother him and he probably wouldn't know anyway if it's being handled by agents."

"Which I should imagine it would be as he's far too busy to think about letting the place."

Lottie entered the room with three mugs of tea and a plate of chocolate digestives on a tray. "I caught the end of what you're saying and you may be right but it's also possible the two men could be colleagues of Brett's. I mean, being in show biz he must have a huge circle of friends and no doubt several would be happy to get away from it all and spend a few days in Cornwall."

"True, or they could even be squatters," said Kitty, "but I hope not."

"Well tomorrow evening when we go down to the village for bingo, we'll take a look to see if there are any cars outside or lights on in the house."

"There were no cars this morning," said Kitty, "I looked as I was leaving Betsy's. That's why I'm a bit concerned."

On Tuesday evening as planned Hetty and Lottie walked down Long Lane and into the village for bingo. They had purposely left home earlier than usual and when they reached the village hall they walked on by towards the church where they could see Sea View Cottage. To avoid it looking as though they were spying on the house, they sat down on the bench in front of the church's boundary wall as though waiting for a bus. There were lights on in the sitting room and in one of the bedrooms. In front of the house a dark coloured four-wheel drive vehicle gleamed in the light from a streetlamp.

"Well," said Hetty, "there's definitely someone there and as they have a car and a new one at that then they're unlikely to be squatters so that's a relief."

Lottie pointed to the upstairs window where the light had gone out. "I agree, so the chances are it's all legal and above board. Strange we've not heard though because Tess being the housekeeper when it changes tenancy likes to keep everyone up to date."

As she spoke the light in the downstairs room also went out and the outside lamp went on. Two young men then emerged from the front door chatting as they walked along the path. The sisters watched as they left the premises, closed the garden gate and then walked along the pavement in a westerly direction.

"Going to the pub do you think?" Hetty asked.

Lottie stood up. "Most likely and if they are we'll see them when we go there after bingo."

When they arrived at the village hall, Debbie was already there. "You're late this week. I was beginning to think you weren't coming. I'd have felt a right numpty playing on my own."

The sisters sat down with their friend and told her where they had been and why.

Later, when they arrived at the pub they found the table by the fire where they liked to sit was taken. Not only was it taken but the persons seated there were the two young men who had earlier left Sea View Cottage. To make matters worse they noted that Tess was not working and that just James and Ella were on the bar.

"So with no Tess how are we going find out who they are?" Lottie hissed.

"By sitting on the table next to them, I suppose," reasoned Hetty. "Nothing like a bit of good old-fashioned eavesdropping."

Debbie frowned. "But we don't like that table because people keep walking by it and it's not very cosy."

"Beggars can't be choosers." Hetty crossed towards the unloved table and unwound the woollen scarf from around her neck. Debbie joined her as Lottie went to the bar for three glasses of wine. When Lottie returned she looked smug and after removing her coat and hanging it on the back of her chair she sat down and nodded in the direction of the two young men. "They're actors," she whispered, "and are here for a break."

Hetty's mouth gaped open. "How do you know that?"

All three ladies leaned forwards so they would not be overheard.

"Ella told me. Well, actually she didn't just tell me, I asked. You see as I approached the bar I heard James say to her that they looked familiar and Ella said it's because they were in a TV drama they'd both watched a while back. I'd never heard of it but when I was being served I asked Ella if they were actors and she said yes. Their names are Gerald and Quincey but I don't know which is which."

"Well done, Lottie," Hetty was impressed.

"And if they're actors they could well be friends of Brett's, him being a script writer, playwright and all that stuff." Debbie sat up straight and took a sip of wine.

"Yes, so that's that mystery solved," Lottie felt relieved, "I'll ring Betsy in the morning and put her mind at rest."

At seven o'clock the following evening, Percy Pickering left his home at number one Hawthorn Road, his destination the Crown and Anchor. As he passed by number thirteen he slowed his pace and looked over the gate towards the empty house. It was in complete darkness; there was no longer any police presence but in the light of a streetlamp he could see that the blue and white tape was still in situ and the grass was worn and flattened where the white tent had recently covered the lawn edges on either side of the garden path to screen the entrance to the house. Percy shuddered. The thought of someone being murdered in Hawthorn Road, his home for many years, filled him with sadness. Eager to get his hands on a pint of cider and hear a few friendly voices he quickened his pace in order to reach his destination.

It was gone eleven when Percy left the Crown and Anchor. He walked part way home with Sid the plumber and they chatted about the demise of Vivien Spencer, the inclement weather, the price of houses in Cornwall and the long running saga of Brexit. When they reached the turning into Honeysuckle Drive, they bade each other goodnight and went their separate ways.

Percy continued along the main street and, as he turned into Goose Lane, he pulled up the collar of his coat to protect his face from the cold fresh wind blowing from the north east. The five pints of cider he had drunk and the fact that Goose Lane rose to higher ground slowed his pace so he was glad when he reached the top of the hill and turned into Hawthorn Road where his house lay at the far end. As he passed number thirteen he quickened his pace; talk of the murder had put him on edge but then something caused him to stop abruptly. From the corner of his eye he saw a flash of light in an upstairs window. Percy retraced his steps and peeped through a gap in the hedge. He thought perhaps it might be the owner of the house, Graham Spencer, but then he remembered that Graham was still in the pub when he had left. He had a full pint of beer and was chatting with other men. Furthermore, he was staying in the pub so would have no reason to visit his house late at night. Unsure what to do, Percy did the unthinkable: he walked through the gate and quietly tip-toed along the path to the back of the house where he hid in the darkness behind a garden shed and watched. Crouched down with his arms crossed to keep warm, his teeth chattered with fear and with cold. When a ginger tom cat meowed and leapt from the top of the shed, he jumped and toppled backwards into the long, damp grass. Cursing beneath his breath he watched as Oscar, equally alarmed, ran off into the neighbouring garden, hissing with his fluffed up tail pointing heavenwards. Composing himself Pickle returned his attention to his surveillance and saw lights flashing in two upstairs rooms. Knowing the layout of the house he realised one torch could not light two rooms at the same time. He stifled a gasp on realising there must be at least two people inside. Recalling the fate of Vivien Spencer and knowing that if he were to be seen he'd be outnumbered, he quickly scrambled to his feet, made his way round to the front of the house and ran all the way home. Once inside he locked and bolted the door and then rang the police.

Chapter Thirteen

On Friday morning, Kitty called in at Primrose Cottage for a chat and it was obvious by the bounce in her step that she had something of interest to share. She began her report before she had even removed her coat.

"Tommy was in the Crown and Anchor last night and he said Pickle was in there telling everyone that on Wednesday night he saw flashing lights as he walked by number thirteen Hawthorn Road. Apparently, he was on his way home from the pub so it was well past eleven. Fair put the wind up him because he knew it wasn't Graham because Graham was in the pub. Anyway, to put his mind at rest he rang the police and asked them to check it out."

"Was Graham in the pub with Charles?" Hetty asked casually to give the impression she was mildly interested but in reality she was longing to know if Charles was still around.

"I've no idea, Het. Tommy didn't say who he was with and I don't expect Pickle would know who Charles is anyway." Kitty hung her coat on the newel post at the foot of the stairs.

"Yes, of course." Hetty felt deflated as they walked into the sitting room.

"So if someone was in the Hawthorn Road house, who might it have been?" Lottie asked as Kitty joined her on the sofa. Hetty meanwhile, to hide her glum face, offered to make coffee and went off into the kitchen.

"Well, that's what I can't make out. Unless it was someone hoping to find something worth pinching to sell at car boots or whatever. Might even have been the same folks as were looking for your vacuum cleaner but I doubt it."

"I suppose so but they'd have been taking a bit of a risk, wouldn't they? I mean, the house was recently a crime scene and there were police everywhere."

Kitty shuddered. "You're right and after what happened to poor Vivien you wouldn't catch me in there for all the tea in China. At least not after dark and on my own."

"Nor me. So did the police go round and check it out, do you know?"

"Yes, they did but it was some time later."

"And I suppose by then whoever it was had long gone."

"I should imagine so. Anyway, Graham went up there yesterday and he said he couldn't see that anything had been taken and that the place looked much the same as when he last went there. Oh, and another thing I've just remembered is that Tommy said Pickle claimed he saw lights flashing in two different rooms at the same time. So he reckoned there had to be at least two people in there."

Hetty entered the room with mugs of coffee and biscuits on a tray. "I could hear what you were saying while I was in the kitchen. So if Pickle saw flashing lights that means someone was definitely in there and that leads me to the question, how then did whoever get in? I'm assuming there are no signs of forced entry this time."

"Oh! I didn't think of that." Kitty was surprised by her own lack of perception.

Lottie laughed. "And if not, perhaps Pickle had had one too many then or he dreamt it."

Kitty took the coffee offered to her, "Thanks, Het," she warmed her hands on the mug, "I still can't believe I was so short-sighted."

"Well, if Pickle's right I can only assume that someone must have a key," Hetty sat down and then dunked a ginger nut in her coffee, "and it was probably even the person who broke in before and killed poor Vivien. You know, he might have grabbed a spare key on his way out. Something like that."

"Meaning, it was always his intention to return at a later date," Lottie said, "Makes sense I suppose because he didn't get much the first time round."

Kitty shuddered. "I wouldn't think after what happened to poor Vivien that whoever would want to set foot in the place ever again. Besides, if he went back hoping to find the fifty thousand pounds he must live on Mars because everyone around here knows it's been found. It even made one of the national papers thanks to young Craig."

"True," agreed Hetty, "but he might have been after something else although I shouldn't think there's much of any great value there now anyway, so why bother?"

Kitty took a sip of coffee. "I agree and whoever broke in needn't have bothered anyway because according to Tommy, Graham Spencer is going home on Sunday after he's had house clearance people in. Meanwhile he's letting it be known that if anyone wants anything from the house then he'll be there all day today and wants people to come and help themselves to as much as they can carry."

Hetty gasped. "What! Why didn't you say so earlier? Drink up, ladies, we must go there right now."

"No way, we'll look like vultures," Lottie was appalled at the idea.

Hetty quickly finished her coffee and placed her empty mug on the tray. "Nonsense. Anyway, we need to see the inside of the house to get some idea of how and what happened. At the moment we're having to guess the layout of the place and imagine the spot where poor Vivien was slain. It's the ideal opportunity."

"Vivien wasn't slain, Het, she was suffocated," scoffed Lottie.

"It's the same difference."

Kitty seemed reluctant to move. "Well whatever, I think I agree with Lottie, Het. I wouldn't want to go in there after what happened whether it'd help our sleuthing efforts or not."

"You really are a couple of spoil sports."

"Perhaps Debbie might like to go with you," suggested Lottie.

Hetty sprang to her feet. "Yes, of course. She's a tough old bird, I'll give her a ring."

Two hours later, Debbie dropped Hetty off at Primrose Cottage along with a stack of plates, a rug, six wine glasses, a footstool, a table lamp, a full-length mirror, a box of CDs, and a bag containing two pairs of curtains.

Hetty waved to Debbie as she drove away and tooted. "You should have been there, Lottie. Lots of people were and still are. Bernie and Veronica were there too. Bernie was helping people load up their cars and vehicles and Veronica was serving tea and cake."

After Hetty had moved everything from the doorstep and into the hallway, she closed the door. "Has Kitty gone?"

"Yes, she went about ten minutes ago."

"A shame because she and Tommy really ought to pop along there because Graham is really appreciative of everyone's help and he said he'd much rather things went to people in the village than have it possibly end up in landfill."

"Yes, there is that I suppose," conceded Lottie, "so did Debbie take much?"

"About the same as me and I've reserved the bookcase Zac first mentioned when he dropped off the vacuum cleaner. It wouldn't fit in Debbie's car so Norman's going to collect it and drop it up later at the same time as he drops off the writing bureau at the Old Bakehouse. I didn't see Bill and Sandra but

Norman said they were there earlier and they loved the look of the bureau."

"So Bill, Sandra and Norman all had a look round." Lottie was beginning to wish she had gone too.

"Yes, loads of people had been and gone and lots were still there. It was quite a social event and I must admit I rather enjoyed it. Daisy and Maisie were there too having closed for lunch and they've taken a few of the smaller items for the charity shop. They didn't want any more wine glasses though because they already have loads. That's why I brought them back. I know we don't need them but they're rather nice." Hetty fetched the footstool from the hallway and placed it on the sitting room floor. From it she took a ruby red wine glass to show her sister.

"Very nice. I hope you didn't get any cushions though."

"Cushions?"

"Yes, remember poor Vivien was suffocated with a cushion."

Hetty sat down heavily on the sofa. "Ugh, I didn't think of that. But looking back on it I'm pretty sure there weren't any cushions there anyway or even a sofa or armchairs for that matter, so somebody had probably already taken them. Having said that, I'm sure the cushion used on Vivien, God rest her soul, would be with the police anyway."

"Yes, I suppose it would. So were you able to visualise how the crime happened?"

"Oh yes. As we know Sid and Zac found Vivien lying on the floor just inside the sitting room and the sitting room door is opposite the bottom of the staircase. We know from Sid that she was in her nightdress and as we've said before she must have heard noises and gone downstairs to investigate. What happened next we can only guess but I should imagine that when she looked into the sitting room, whoever was there would be ready and waiting having heard her coming down the stairs. Why he felt it was necessary to kill her though I've no idea unless it turned out they knew each other but I think that's unlikely because she didn't live in the village, did she? And so for that reason she can't have known many people. I mean, we never clapped eyes on her, did we?"

"No we didn't and I think we're wasting our time looking for an individual as the chances are there was more than one. Remember, Pickle reckons that was the case the other night when he saw flashing lights. In fact the more I think about it, the more I think we should be looking for a gang and not an individual or even a couple."

"A gang!" Hetty chuckled, "I can't imagine a gang of crooks working in Pentrillick."

"Why not?"

"Well, umm…I don't really know but it just seems silly."

"Humph! I don't see why."

"It's just a thought, but I wonder if the person or persons involved might actually live in Hawthorn Road. I mean, if they did it's possible they'd have seen Vivien at some point and could even have become acquainted with her. They might also have known Nigel Taylor and, remember, whoever it was that Pickle saw in the house must have had a key."

"Or as we said earlier, stolen a key first time round," Lottie placed her hands on her lap. "It's certainly food for thought although I'm sure the police will have questioned the neighbours and I've just remembered it's said that the next door neighbours kept an eye on the house over Christmas and New Year and switched on lights each night to make it look like someone was there."

"Ah, yes they did which means they must have had a key and even if they gave it back which I expect they did, they could have had a copy made beforehand."

Lottie shook her head. "No, that doesn't make sense, Het. I mean why would they break in after Vivien got back when they'd had access to the place over the Christmas period? They could have searched the place thoroughly from top to toe in that time and cleared up any mess they made."

Hetty's exhilaration diminished. "So back to the drawing board then."

"Unless we can think of anyone else who lives in Hawthorn Road, then yes."

"Which I can't, other than Pickle, that is and we can't really claim to know him. I mean, we know who he is and we've spoken to him before but we know very little about him other than the fact that he's a widower and has two grown up children but neither live in the village."

"And that he's been there for years. Meaning he must know most of the people in that road."

Hetty tapped her nails on her teeth. "You're right, Lottie. So how can we get chatting to him?"

"I don't know. It'd look odd if we suddenly struck up a conversation with him."

"Well, we'll have to come up with a plan of some sort because questioning him is the only way I can see of finding out who else lives along that road."

"I agree and to help, I think next time we see Debbie and Kitty that'll have to be our main topic of conversation."

On Sunday evening the sisters went to the Crown and Anchor for quiz night and during the interval, Hetty spotted Pickle standing at the far end of the bar talking to Sid. He had his back to the table where the ladies sat. Seeing the opportunity to speak to him, Hetty stood up and grabbed her handbag. "Be back shortly."

To the surprise of her quiz mates, she dashed off to the Ladies. As she passed Pickle on her way back she deliberately stumbled causing him to spill a little of his drink.

"Oh, I'm so sorry, Pickle. It's my silly right leg, it sometimes gives way and I stumble." Hetty sounded very convincing.

"Don't worry, love. No harm done."

"But I've spilled some of your drink. Please let me get you another."

"No, no need for that. It was only a dribble."

"But I insist. Be back in a minute." Hetty went to the bar. Tess was free and she asked for a pint of whatever Pickle was drinking.

"Pickle?" Queried Tess.

"Yes," Hetty winked.

With a chuckle, Tess poured a pint of Pickle's favourite cider.

"You shouldn't have," said Pickle, as she handed him a full glass.

"It's the least I can do. From what I've heard you had a bit of a fright the other night on your way home from here."

"Ah, the flashing lights in number thirteen, you mean? Yes, they fair put the wind up me. Goodness knows what that was about though because Graham reckoned nothing had been taken. I'll be glad when the place is sold and lived in again. It gives me the creeps standing empty."

"I'll second that," said Sid, "I'm not one to get spooked, but that house felt uncomfortable. I even thought the same when I popped along to Graham's clear out."

"Really?" Hetty was surprised, "I thought the atmosphere was rather nice especially with tea and cake on offer but then I wasn't the one who found poor Vivien. Nor do I live in Hawthorn Road."

Pickle chuckled. "You're lucky there."

"Yes, it can't be very nice for any of you after what happened, and I suppose your neighbours in Hawthorn Road feel the same."

"You're right they do and especially the ones on either side of thirteen. I was chatting to Tim Rudd who lives next door the other day and he said it's made Susan very nervous. She jumps every time she hears an unfamiliar noise now."

"Did um anyone of them see or hear anything on the night Vivien was murdered?" Hetty's fingers were crossed behind her back.

"No not really. Tim said Susan heard a few strange noises while she was reading. He was asleep at the time so didn't see or hear anything, but Susan who likes to read to make herself sleepy was still awake. Anyway, just after midnight she popped to the loo and when she was on her way back from the bathroom she heard a door slam. Out of curiosity she looked out the window and saw two blokes get into a car and drive off at a fair pace, but whether that was anything to do with the break in is anyone's guess. I mean, a lot of the youngsters drive too fast these days so it could have been someone's mate going home or summat like that. I 'spect the coppers checked it out anyway but I don't really know any more than that."

"Hmm. Any idea what type of car it was?" Hetty wished she was acquainted with the Rudds but as far as she knew she'd never clapped eyes on them.

"No, but it was a dark colour."

"And four-wheel drive," Sid added, "I know that because when the coppers questioned me, they wanted to know what type of vehicle I drove."

Hetty looked at Sid. "So, were you a suspect?"

"Briefly, yes."

"Ridiculous."

Sid chuckled. "Thank you. I appreciate your loyalty."

"You're welcome and it's just occurred to me that if the driver of the four-wheel thingy *was* responsible for killing Vivien, it means they can't live nearby or they would have walked, wouldn't they."

Pickle finished his original pint and put the empty glass on the bar. "Good point, which I must admit is a bit of comfort to me, especially as I live on my own."

"Did you know Nigel at all?" Hetty asked.

Pickle shook his head. "No, he didn't mix with the likes of us and I can't say that I ever saw much of him. He never even came in here for a pint. Having said that he must have gone somewhere boozing because twice when I was walking home from here, I saw him stumble up the garden path into number thirteen and then fumble around trying to get the key in the lock. It was quite amusing. He didn't know I was there as I watched him through the hedge on both occasions. I must admit, I had a bit of a chuckle."

"Really! Anyway, I must get back to the others because it looks like James is about to start the second half of the quiz. Been nice talking to you, Pickle. And you Sid."

"Likewise," Pickle raised his fresh pint, "and thanks for the drink."

"Did you learn anything?" Debbie asked before Hetty had a chance to sit down.

"Not really. Other than the fact someone in the house next door to thirteen saw a four-wheel drive vehicle with two people inside leave Hawthorn Road just after twelve on the night that Vivien died."

"That's interesting and at least we now know what type of vehicle the bad guys drive," Lottie pointed to a glass of red wine, "We bought you another drink by the way while you were interrogating Pickle."

"Thank you," she took a sip, "Oh well I didn't learn very much but having heard about the vehicle I think we can safely say that no-one along Hawthorn Road is or was involved in any of the occurrences."

Debbie picked up her pen ready to continue writing down the team's quiz answers. "I agree and if the two blokes Mrs

Rudd saw are the ones who broke into number thirteen it would really help if we knew what they were actually looking for."

"Well whatever, it isn't in the writing bureau that's for sure," said Bill, emphatically, "I've had all the drawers out and turned it upside down and there are no secret hidey holes or stuff like that."

"Not that we really expected there would be," Sandra added. "No, more's the shame."

"So, the only thing we know for sure is that we're looking for people who must have known Nigel well but for the life of me I can't think who that might be." Kitty unwrapped a bar of chocolate and offered it around the table.

"Or an individual," said Hetty, taking a piece of chocolate, "who roped in a friend or two. But whatever, I don't think he or they live in Pentrillick."

Chapter Fourteen

Inside the police station, officers gathered to mull over the known facts of the Hawthorn Road murder case.

DCI Worthington, an officer recently transferred to the Devon and Cornwall Police Force from Gloucestershire summed up the salient points.

"It's estimated that Vivien Spencer died between 10pm and midnight on Tuesday January the seventh. Wounds on the back of her head indicate she was forcibly knocked to the floor and was then suffocated. Fibres found on a cushion matched those found on her face. The last person she spoke to was her husband who rang her at ten that evening when she told him of the day's events. This means the time of death is more likely to be between 11pm and midnight. The last persons to see her alive were plumbers, Zac Burton and Sidney Moore who left the house in Hawthorn Road at 5pm. Mr Moore and Mr Burton have both been questioned and released without charge.

Mrs Susan Rudd who lives next door heard noises coming from number thirteen shortly after midnight. When she heard a door slam, she looked from the bedroom window and saw two figures run across the road. They hurriedly drove away in a four-wheel drive vehicle in a southerly direction towards Goose Lane. The vehicle was dark in colour but because of the artificial light from the streetlamps the colour cannot be ratified. Mrs Rudd did not get the registration number because she was not wearing her spectacles.

The persons who broke into number thirteen gained access through the back door by reaching up through the cat flap for the key still in the lock. It's assumed they believed the house to be empty and so were surprised when they were disturbed by Mrs Spencer who was sleeping in one of the bedrooms and must have gone downstairs to investigate probable noises.

It is assumed the intruders were looking for something and no doubt the money which has since been found in a vacuum cleaner taken from the house earlier that day. According to Sidney Moore, he saw Mr Taylor's mobile phone and laptop on top of a writing bureau. This was pointed out to him and his apprentice, Zac Burton, by the deceased who didn't know what to do with them. When Mrs Spencer's body was found they were no longer on the bureau or anywhere else in the house and so we must assume they were taken during the raid. This means we've been unable to establish any friends and contacts of Mr Taylor other than his sister whose details were provided to us by Mr Spencer who had her listed as the next of kin. And before you ask, we've found no evidence to suggest that Mr Taylor engaged in any social media activity and as he and his sister had not been in contact for five years or more, she was unable to tell us anything of his life here in Cornwall. We had hoped to find a diary or even a good old-fashioned address book but our searches have found neither, therefore we can only assume that details of any contacts Mr Taylor had were confined to his laptop and phone.

We questioned Mr and Mrs Dale, the licensees at the Crown and Anchor in Pentrillick and neither knew or ever met Nigel Taylor, therefore, we assume that he socialised and drank elsewhere. We've questioned his neighbours, but it appears he didn't associate with any of them, however, several claim to have seen him on occasion arriving home a little unsteady on his feet. We need to know where he drank. Was it in a pub elsewhere or was it at the home of an associate? If it was a pub elsewhere then how did he get back to Pentrillick? Local taxi firms have been questioned but to date none recall ever dropping off Mr Taylor in Hawthorn Road. We need to know who he associated with and whether anyone ever heard him speak of money hidden at his home.

Finally, we were informed of lights seen inside number thirteen on Wednesday last between eleven pm and midnight. We investigated but there was no sign of a forced entry and nothing appears to have been taken. Mr Spencer has since confirmed that there had been two keys for the back door and only one now remains on the keyring. We assume therefore that the persons who broke into the house on the night Mrs Spencer was killed must have taken the second key to enable them to return. What exactly they were looking for on the return visit is a mystery."

At the end of the report Detective Inspector Fox thanked DCI Worthington and addressed the officers. "Any questions?"

A young police sergeant raised her hand. "Are we sure that the two plumbers who found the body are not involved?"

"Yes. The younger of the two, Mr Burton has an alibi. He was home with his girlfriend. His mother is also able to ratify this as she called in after ten o'clock when she finished her shift in the nearby care home and was there for approximately one hour. The other, Mr Moore, lives alone and therefore has no alibi but he does not own a dark coloured four-wheel drive and Mr Spencer says his wife was satisfied that the plumbers were reliable and honest. In fact, she raved about their workmanship and their good nature as recently as the phone call on the night she died. Furthermore, both were left alone for a couple of hours during the morning of her death when she visited the charity shop and a supermarket and so would have had ample time to search the property and take anything they wanted then. We're confident that neither knew about the money because neither knew or had ever met Nigel Taylor."

"How about her husband?" the sergeant asked, "Is he in the clear?"

"Yes. He spoke to his wife from the landline at his home in Devon at ten o'clock in a call that lasted for twenty minutes. This has been ratified and so there would have been insufficient time for him to have driven to Cornwall."

"Do we have descriptions of the two people who were seen driving away on the night Mrs Spencer was murdered?"

"Nothing helpful I'm afraid. Both wore dark clothing and appeared to be of average height and build. Could be just about anyone. Although they moved pretty quickly so I'd say they were agile."

"Have we looked through the list of people who attended his funeral in order to establish any friends and associates?"

"If only that were possible but there has been no funeral. Mr Taylor left his body to medical research and asked that when his remains were no longer of any use he be cremated and his ashes be forwarded to his sister to dispose of by a method of her choosing."

That same day, Sid and Zac returned to number thirteen Hawthorn Road. The floors were bare and the house was completely empty, its last items having been taken away by a house clearance team on Saturday. As they went inside and closed the door their voices and movements echoed.

Sid looked around the empty sitting room. No fire burned in the grate. No cat sat on the hearth rug. No smell of coffee emanated from the kitchen and the Christmas cake had no doubt long gone. "Bit different to when we first came here. I must admit I've really got that Monday morning feeling today and I shan't be sorry to finish this job. Now it's empty it gives me the creeps and as I said to Pickle and your Auntie Hetty last night, I'm not usually one to get spooked."

Zac tightly folded his arms across his chest. "I am though so do you think we could get it done this week?"

"I don't see why not and with the place being empty there's nothing to distract us. It's bloomin' cold in here though."

"It is," Zac pulled up the zip on his jacket to his chin, "I heard Vivien's husband is going to sell this place now rather than let it out again."

"That's right, he is. He rang on Saturday night to say that everything had been cleared out and when we're done, he's going to put it on the market. Can't say as I blame him. This place will always have bad memories for him and for us as well," Sid looked at the empty hearth, "Hard to imagine the place warm with a glowing fire and the sound of laughter as there must have been over the years."

Zac shuddered as he recalled the day they had found Vivien Spencer. "So, when is Norman coming in to give the place a lick of paint?"

"Not sure but according to Graham he'll be here this week some time."

As he spoke, they heard a key turn in the front door lock followed by footsteps in the hallway.

"Are you here, Sid, Zac? Please say yes."

Sid looked around the door. "Yes, we are, Norm, and we were just talking about you. Are you making a start today?"

"Yes, I am and thank goodness you're here. I saw Graham on Friday afternoon when he was giving stuff away. We got chatting and he said he'd appreciate it done as soon as possible as he's going to sell the place." Norman shuddered, "He said you'd both be here so I'd not be alone which is just as well as the place feels creepy."

"And it's made worse by having no furniture," Sid nodded to Oscar by who had followed Norman in, "I see you've made a friend?"

Norman tutted. "Yes, I'm told he lives next door and used to belong to Nigel. For some reason he seems to have taken a liking to me. It was the same when I was here collecting furniture the other day. I think he could smell the tuna I'd fed to Muffins. Got a smashing couple of single beds by the way. Just what we wanted." Norman looked around the bare room, "I think I'll get my radio from the van when I bring in the paint and try and liven things up a bit."

"Where will you be starting?" Sid asked.

"The bedrooms. I like to start at the top and work my way down."

"Ideal, you'll be up near us then so we can all keep each other company."

"Daffodils," said Hetty as Debbie arrived at Primrose Cottage on Tuesday morning and handed the over the flowers. "They're beautiful, thank you. Are they from your garden?"

"No, not many of mine are out yet. I bought these from the shop on my way here. They were in a bucket in the doorway and it says they're grown locally."

"Probably from Willow Farm then. You know, the Glovers' place. Might even have been picked by either Gus or Tony."

"Gus and Tony?" Debbie appeared nonplussed.

"Yes, you know, the two chaps that Kitty knows. We saw them in the pub the other day."

"Oh, yes, I remember." Debbie removed her coat as Hetty closed the door. "Lottie's in there. Go in and make yourself at home while I pop these in water and put the kettle on."

Debbie went into the sitting room. "Morning, Lottie. Ow, it strikes lovely and warm in here."

"Nice to see you, Debs, but you look frozen." Lottie laid her knitting down on the floor by her feet.

Debbie warmed her hands by the fire. "I am. I walked here today, you see, because I thought I needed the exercise and despite wearing fleecy lined boots my feet are still like blocks of ice."

Hetty entered the room with the flowers in a white vase. "Look at these, Lottie. Debbie brought them for us, aren't they beautiful?"

"They are. I love seeing the first daffodils. They make me think that spring's just around the corner even though it's not really."

Hetty went back out and returned with three mugs on a tray and a plate piled with slices of buttered fruit loaf and chocolate biscuits.

Lottie took a sip of coffee; it was too hot, so she placed it on the occasional table beside the sofa. "We're glad you're here, Debbie because we've come up with a plan, haven't we, Het?"

"You have? Now that sounds exciting."

"It could be," Hetty smiled at the thought of their idea, "and it'll be a bit of fun even if it's unproductive because it's nice to get out of the village now and again."

Debbie picked up her slice of fruit loaf. "I'm intrigued. Please tell me more."

Lottie continued. "Well, last night Bill rang after he got back from the pub. It was quite late but he decided to ring anyway hoping that we were still up. Because after witnessing Het's stage managed questioning of Pickle on Sunday night he realised we're still as keen as ever to solve any little mysteries that come our way. For that reason he felt that what he'd heard might be of use to us. You see, there was a pool match on in the pub last night and our lot were playing a team from the Nag's Head in Penzance. Bill was sitting at the bar with Norman when during their break one of the Nag's team ordered a drink. The Nag's man and James got chatting and the name Nigel Taylor cropped up. Needless to say Bill's ears started flapping especially when the Nag's chap told James that Nigel was a great mate of the landlord there and so was a regular. So you see, Het and I figure that if we were to pop over to the Nag's Head we might be able to get some idea of who drinks there and see if we think any of them might have broken into number thirteen after poor Nigel died and nicked his phone and laptop while they were there."

"And killed Vivien," Hetty added.

"Well, yes, of course. That goes without saying."

Debbie frowned. "Nag's Head. Isn't that the pub where the reporter chappie had been drinking before he was run down?"

Hetty slapped her own forehead. "How did we miss that fact, Lottie? Of course it is. What a couple of nitwits we are."

Lottie tutted. "You know I had a feeling I'd heard the name before, but it just didn't register. Thank goodness one of us is still sharp."

Debbie preened, flattered by Lottie's complimentary words. "Anyway, going there will serve a double purpose. We might not only find out something about the chap who killed poor Vivien but also learn what Craig was doing there and who he spoke to."

"Killing two birds with one stone as they say," Lottie brushed biscuit crumbs from her lap into her hand and dropped them onto the tray, "although I hate that phrase."

Hetty nodded. "So do I. Poor birds."

"Well whatever, I think going to the Nag's Head is an absolutely brilliant idea so count me in."

Hetty chuckled. "We thought you'd like it."

"I most certainly do. So when shall we go?"

"The sooner the better," said Hetty, "It's time we had something to get our teeth into and we're not going to find the answers sitting here by the fire: that's for sure."

Lottie waved her hand in an easterly direction. "And we'll get Kitty to come along as well. The more pairs of ears and eyes, the more we'll hear and see."

"Have you mentioned it to her yet?"

Hetty stood up. "No, but now we've told you and got your approval I'll give her a ring."

"That was quick," said Lottie, when her sister returned to the room in less than two minutes.

"That's because Kitty's coming down here so we can thrash out the details. She sounded quite excited and said she was on her way."

After an hour, a second cup of coffee and more biscuits and slices of fruit loaf, the ladies had come up with a plan. That being they would go to bingo as usual that evening and then visit the Nag's Head the following night. They pondered over whether to go on the bus, take a taxi or one of them drive and eventually decided to go on the bus and then either catch one home again or get Gideon to pick them up.

"Does anyone know where the Nag's Head is?" Hetty asked, "Because I've just realised that I don't have the foggiest idea. In fact, when Bill rang, Lottie and I thought we'd never even heard of it but we now know we had because of the Craig connection. Does that make sense?"

"Just about," said Kitty, "and to answer your question I've no idea where it is either."

Debbie shook her head. "Likewise."

"I remember hearing the name of the road on the news report about Craig," said Lottie, "but having never heard it before it went in one ear and out the other."

"I'll Google it," Debbie took her phone from her handbag.

Hetty, Lottie and Kitty waited patiently.

"Ah, it's in Wesley Road. There's a map here and it looks like it should be easy to find."

"Wesley Road, yes that rings a bell," said Hetty, "although I've no idea where it is."

"Is it anywhere near the bus station?" Kitty asked, "We don't want to be walking far through the town especially after dark."

Debbie gave the question a little thought before she answered. "Judging by the map I'd say it's about a ten to fifteen minutes' walk from there."

"No problem then," said Lottie, "we're used to walking and don't worry about the dark, Kitty, there's safety in numbers."

Kitty nodded. "True and I like walking anyway although I don't walk as much as I used to but I certainly like to get out every day unless the weather's really foul."

While she had her phone out Debbie checked bus times. "Right, the buses are every hour at a quarter past so we'll either need to catch the six fifteen or the seven fifteen. What do you think?"

The ladies were unanimous and opted for the six fifteen.

"The earlier we get there the better," said Hetty with glee.

In the evening the ladies went to bingo in the village hall as usual and then to the Crown and Anchor where Hetty was pleased to see that Charles was still in the village. On her way back from a visit to the Ladies she casually greeted him. He stood and took her hand.

"I've been meaning to ask you, Henrietta, how you and your sister came to be living in Cornwall."

"It's quite simple. We came down for a holiday in 2016 with Lottie's son and his family. We fell in love with the village, both sold our individual houses, bought one here to share and were back here in time for Christmas."

"That's fascinating. So what became of Charlotte's husband? I believe she married Hugh Burton. Is that correct?"

"Yes, she did but Hugh died several months before the holiday. That's partly why we were asked by the family to join them. Bill and Sandra thought Lottie needed to get away, you see. And I was retired so was footloose and fancy free."

"Ah, yes, that makes sense."

"And of course since then Bill and his family have moved to Cornwall as well and so they're also in the village. They live at the Old Bakehouse along the main street." Hetty pointed towards the bar. "That's Lottie's son Bill there. The chap sitting on the stool wearing a grey top."

Charles' jaw dropped. "Good gracious. He looks very much like his father."

"Yes, Hugh was a very handsome man." Hetty turned back to face her old flame, "So, what about you, Charles? Where are you living now?"

"In Kensington. I left Northamptonshire about twenty years ago to join a prestigious practice. Private of course."

"Well I never. So, you're a city boy now."

Charles smiled broadly showing off his perfectly straight gleaming white teeth. "Indeed I am."

Hetty wondered if the teeth were false. "Do you regret leaving the countryside for city life?"

"No, never. I love the buzz of the city and doubt I shall ever tire of it. As Samuel Johnson said: When a man is tired of London, he is tired of life."

Hetty laughed. "You must be finding Cornwall in the winter very dull then."

"Not at all. I like the contrast and am very much enjoying my stay," he stroked her cheek, "and the company."

Chapter Fifteen

"Off globetrotting again?" Norman pointed over the garden fence between the two houses to Polly's suitcase as she placed it in the boot of her car.

"Yes, tough old job but someone has to do it."

"Get away with you. You love it."

"You're right, I do."

"You'll probably think me a bit of a Luddite, but I've never flown anywhere. In fact, I've never been out of the country in any mode of transport."

Polly closed the boot. "Tut tut, you should try it sometime, Norman. You'd love it. There's a big wide world out there."

"Hmm, maybe, we'll see. There's not anywhere that I particularly want to go to though. I used to think I'd like to visit Switzerland and try my hands at skiing but not anymore. Far too old now."

"You're never too old, Norman."

"You think that now but you wait and see. You get to a stage in life when you realise that you don't bounce anymore. Anyway, that's enough about age, how long are you off for this time?"

"Only five days. So I'll be back before you know it. Home for three days then off again after that for six days."

"Be one big party for Jay then."

Polly laughed. "That might have been the case before we had Barnaby but now he assures me he'll spend most of his time painting and taking the hound for walks."

An image flashed across Norman's mind of Jay's most recent painting. He wanted to say he could knock out something similar in less than ten minutes but instead said, "And probably most of their walks will be to the pub."

"No doubt about that. I think Barnaby could find his way there without either of us."

Norman pulled a bunch of keys from his pocket. "Did Jay get anything interesting at the number thirteen giveaway? I saw him there."

"A few bits but nothing to shout about. We didn't know anything about it and Jay only found out by chance when he popped in the pub for a pint at lunch time. After he finished his drink he went straight up there and said the first person he saw was you loading up a couple of beds in your van."

"That's right, they're in our spare bedroom now. Your Jay arrived just in time to give Bernie and me a hand with them. I got several other interesting things too. Of course, I had the advantage of being in the know because Graham mentioned it to me when we got chatting about me painting the walls."

Polly closed the door of her boot. "I think it was very generous of him to give everything away. Jay said he wouldn't take a penny off anyone."

"That's because he got most of it for a song in the first place. He and Vivien bought the house and its contents from someone whose elderly relative had died and so I don't think he was out of pocket by much."

"Ah, that makes sense then."

"Your camellia's looking good. I reckon it likes it there."

"We're thrilled to bits with it. It's smothered in buds so will be a picture in a day or two. It's inspired me and I'm looking forward to the spring now so I can get more stuff planted."

"Same here. That's the trouble with new places there's nothing but grass and a few weeds. Mind you, I like gardening and Jackie's artistic so we can only improve ours."

Polly smiled. "You never know, if we put the work in our front gardens might be worthy of entering the Pentrillick in Bloom competition that I've heard so much about."

"I don't know about that, but I suppose it's possible. Anyway, I better get off and do a bit of painting. Been nice talking to you, Polly and you take care." Norman unlocked the door of his van.

"Are you still working at the Hawthorn Road house then?"

"Yes, and should have it done in a couple of days."

"Hmm, rather you than me after what happened there. Jay said it felt creepy even with lots of people walking around."

Norman shuddered. "I know just what he means."

Both then climbed into their respective vehicles and drove out of the estate into the lane.

At the bottom of the hill, Norman tooted as Polly turned right at the junction. He then turned left and drove through the village towards Hawthorn Road.

After she had washed the breakfast dishes, Hetty carried the small container they kept outside the back door for vegetable waste down to the end of the garden where they kept the compost bin. As she emptied the box and replaced the bin's lid, she saw two figures strolling across the field that ran along the back of the houses in Blackberry Way. Intrigued as to who they might be she watched their movements. Once they were near enough for Hetty to see their faces she realised they were Tony and Gus the two nomadic daffodil pickers. When they saw her watching them, they waved and crossed to the boundary wall to speak to her.

"Is that Kitty and Tommy's house?" Tony pointed to the rear view of Tuzzy-Muzzy, the first house along Blackberry Way.

"No, no, they live at the other end at Meadowside. That's Chloe and Colin's place next door to us. It's a guest house."

"Ah, that makes sense then. Kitty told us they lived in a modest house at the end of Blackberry Way and we were obviously looking at the wrong end." Gus stepped back a few paces so that he could see the far end of the row of houses.

"So how come you're up here." Hetty was intrigued as the field they stood in was a grass meadow left for a natural habitat of wildlife.

Tony pointed back across the hedgerows. "We're working back there two fields away and when we stopped for a tea break, we decided to nip over here to see if we could see Kitty and Tommy's place. They were telling us about it the other day, you see. And we were curious, that's all."

Gus nodded. "It was Jimmy Glover who pointed the houses out or we wouldn't have known where we were."

"I see," Hetty looked to the sky, "at least you've a nice day for picking daffodils."

"We have and we better get back as we said we'd only be gone ten minutes."

Hetty watched as they marched away. She then picked up the waste vegetable container and returned indoors.

The Glovers' farm was roughly a mile away from the centre of the village; named Willow Farm it had been the family home of the Glover family for over two hundred years. Since the death of his parents in the late nineteen eighties, Jimmy Glover, his wife Tamsin and their twenty-one-year-old son Ryan had run the place with the help of casual labourers and their full time employee, Simon Nance. The granite-built farmhouse lay in a valley surrounded by rolling hills. Its main source of income was from daffodils in the winter months, wheat, sweetcorn, main crop potatoes in the summer and the brassica family through the autumn. The only animals they kept were chickens for their eggs and goats for their milk from which they made cheese.

On Wednesday morning after Tamsin had cleared away the breakfast dishes, washed up and collected the eggs for the day she quickly dusted around the living room and vacuumed the floor. She had taken a little more pride in the room since they had thrown away their old threadbare three-piece suite. Admittedly the one they had acquired from number thirteen Hawthorn Road was a little shabby but at least it was intact and its condition mattered very little for the farm dogs and cats sat on the furniture more frequently than she or her husband.

When the room was clean she went upstairs to make the beds. As she walked along the landing she looked from the window and out across the fields. January was by no means her favourite month but the fields when full of golden daffodils never ceased to delight her.

Back downstairs she made her way into the kitchen to empty the flip-top bin and put out the rubbish for collection the following morning. As she pulled a new black bin liner from a roll her eye was distracted by a guitar case tucked between the dresser and an old Windsor chair. Quickly, she pushed the new liner into the bin and replaced the lid, then lifted up the guitar case and placed it on the solid pine table. Tamsin's husband, Jimmy, had brought back the guitar from number thirteen Hawthorn Road when he and their son Ryan had picked up the three-piece suite. Jimmy knew his wife had always wanted to play and so thought she might appreciate it, but to date, because she had been more concerned with rearranging the living room furniture, she had done nothing more than take a peep inside the battered black case.

Tamsin lifted out the guitar. It had two broken strings and looked as though it had seen better days. However, she was convinced that with a little tender loving care and a new set of strings it'd be as good as new and certainly good enough for her to learn on. All she needed was to find someone able to teach her to play. Conscious that she had work to do in the dairy, she decided to leave the restoration project until the evening when she had more time, but before she packed away the instrument she went through a few sheets of music laying in the bottom of the case to see if there was anything she recognised. Amongst the papers was a thin notebook. Tamsin flicked through its pages. It contained nothing other than names, addresses and telephone numbers. Realising it must have belonged to the late Nigel Taylor and that he would no longer be in need of it, she tossed it into the bag of rubbish then returned the guitar to its case and placed it back beside the dresser. Once done she tied up the top of the full bin liner, took it outside and dropped it into the wheelie bin. She then wheeled the rubbish down to the farm gate for collection the next day accompanied by her favourite dog, Bramble.

Chapter Sixteen

On Wednesday evening, the ladies prepared for their visit to the Nag's Head in Penzance. The weather was dry but cold and so Kitty, Lottie and Hetty wrapped up well and pulled up their collars as they walked briskly down Long Lane where they were to meet Debbie at the bus stop. To their relief she was there ready and waiting; the bus was on time and they arrived at the bus station in Penzance at twenty minutes to seven.

Wesley Road was a back street in a residential area and due to Debbie's research the ladies found it with ease. When they arrived at the Nag's Head they waited outside to weigh up the situation before they crossed the threshold.

"I hope we won't be the only females in there. It looks a bit rough from the outside." Lottie's comment was based on an overflowing ashtray balanced on the granite sill of a wooden window with missing putty and flaking blue paint. On the pavement beneath it, cigarette butts, soggy due to rain, lay beside a tub of long dead summer bedding plants.

Debbie stepped back onto the long straight road where terraced houses lined the street interrupted only by a chapel further down on the opposite side to the pub. Cars were parked on both sides for as far as the eye could see and the narrow pavements were devoid of pedestrians. "I take your point, Lottie, but then it is January and nowhere looks very smart this time of the year."

"True," Lottie had moved closer and was looking through the window, "but you'd think they'd find the time to take the Christmas tree out."

Debbie stepped back onto the pavement and stood by Lottie's side so as to see an artificial tree standing in a dimly lit corner.

"Well at least they've taken the lights and decorations off and it's probably just standing there 'til someone puts it in the loft or whatever."

"Hmm, that's if it ever had lights and decorations on it."

"Well, I just hope it's clean in there," said Hetty, "especially the glasses."

The cold wind blowing along the street caused the ladies to pluck up the courage to make an entrance. As they walked into the bar the chat amongst the few men inside ceased and all eyes of those present followed the ladies as they sat down at the first table they came to.

"Why didn't we bring one of the men with us?" Debbie hissed.

Hetty took her purse from her bag. "Because we didn't think of it. I'll get the drinks."

Debbie, Lottie and Kitty sat down around the table; all felt very conspicuous.

"At least they have an open fire and it's nice and warm in here," whispered Lottie.

Debbie rubbed her hand across the table top. "And this is clean. No rings made by glasses or sticky patches."

Only one person worked on the bar, a man in his fifties. Whether or not he was the landlord and therefore friend of the late Nigel Taylor, Hetty had no idea. She asked for four large glasses of red wine in a friendly manner. When the bartender smiled she felt herself relax. "Merlot or shiraz, my love?" he asked.

Surprised there was a choice, Hetty asked for merlot and watched as he poured the wine into spotlessly clean glasses.

When Hetty returned with the drinks the men resumed their chat having deemed the ladies to be of no interest. The ladies then began to scrutinise the men present to see if any looked sinister or vaguely familiar.

"We should have sat nearer to them so we could eavesdrop," whispered Kitty, "I can't hear a thing back here."

"Nor can I and sitting beneath that speaker's not helping." Lottie glanced up where country music rang from a small speaker attached to a wooden beam.

"Let's move over there then nearer the fire," said Debbie.

The ladies picked up their glasses and belongings and moved to a table in the corner. To give the impression they had moved because they felt cold, Hetty stood in front of the fire briefly on pretence of needing to warm her hands. She then removed her coat and hung it on the back of her chair.

To their disappointment, the men at the nearest table were talking about football. At another a man alone was reading a newspaper and two men at the table furthest away were looking at something on a mobile phone.

"I think we're wasting our time," hissed Lottie.

Hetty looked at a clock above the bar. "It's not even half past seven yet. I'm sure there will be more people in soon."

"So what exactly are we hoping to see?" Kitty took a small sip of wine, licked her lips and then took another.

"Anyone who we think might have known Nigel," said Debbie, "or who appears to be nosy and therefore might have overheard him telling of the fifty thousand pounds. Not that I know what a nosy person looks like."

"I do," chuckled Hetty, "I see one every time I look in our bathroom mirror."

"Perhaps one of us ought to get chatting to the landlord," suggested Lottie, "after all according to Bill he was a friend of Nigel's."

"If he is the landlord," said Hetty, "we just don't know, do we? He might be a member of staff and the landlord has the night off."

At that moment the door opened and in strolled Tony and Gus the daffodil pickers from Glovers' farm; with them were four more young men.

"Yay, two friendly faces," Kitty was genuinely pleased to see them. When she caught Gus's eye, she waved.

While Tony and his colleagues bought their drinks, Gus walked towards the ladies. "Didn't expect to see you in here. Fancied a change of scenery, did you?"

"Well, yes and no. We've been in the town all afternoon um shopping and thought we'd pop in here for a drink before we went home," Kitty lied.

Gus looked at the floor. "No bags, so didn't see anything you liked then?"

Kitty felt her face burning.

Hetty came to the rescue. "The shopping's in the car, Gus. So did you fancy a change of scenery as well?"

"No, well yes I suppose. The thing is we often pop in here. We stumbled across it quite by chance the first winter we picked daffs for the Glovers. We liked the place and so treat it as our second local while we're in Cornwall. It's nice to vary one's drinking holes."

"And are the lads you're with from the farm too?" Hetty asked.

"Yes, like us they're here every year. They come from Poland and are really nice blokes. We often meet up in different locations over the year." Gus saw that Tony had their drinks, "Anyway, nice to see you all. We're going to have a few games of darts now."

"Nice to see you too," said Kitty.

Debbie giggled as he walked away. "Quick thinking there, ladies."

Hetty bit her bottom lip. "It won't be if they ask for a lift back to Pentrillick."

"They won't," reasoned Lottie, "because with four of us we'd already be a car full. That's if we had a car here of course."

As the evening wore on a few more people arrived, the ladies bought another round of drinks and when a loud voiced man arrived they heard him call the bartender, Reg.

"Ah, Reg," whispered Lottie, "Now all we need to know is if that's the name of the landlord."

"No problem there," Hetty stood up, put on her coat and grabbed her handbag.

Debbie frowned. "What do you mean and where are you going?"

"Not far. I'll pop outside so it looks like I'm going out for a fag. While there I'll look to see the name of the licensee. It's bound to be above the door as I think it's the law."

Hetty was gone for as long as she thought it would take to smoke a cigarette. When she returned they saw that she was smiling.

She sat down. "It's freezing out there but he's our boy. Landlord, Reginald Whittle."

"Good work, Het," said Debbie, "Now what do we do?"

Hetty removed her coat. "Watch and wait. I'm sure the opportunity to find something out will arise soon."

Twenty minutes later, Hetty saw that there was no-one at the bar and the landlord was straightening bottles on a shelf and singing along with Dolly Parton. Hetty sprang to her feet. "Quick, drink up ladies, I need to go to the bar."

"I can't drink another," groaned Kitty, "I've already had more than I should. One's my limit when it comes to red wine and I've had two."

"I'll get you a tonic water then. Which is a good idea anyway as we need it to look as though one of us is a driver."

"You can't have another either, Het. Your New Year's resolution was to have no more than two glasses of wine a night." Lottie drained her glass and placed it on the table beside Debbie's.

Hetty picked up the empty glasses. "There are times, Lottie Burton when one has to sacrifice one's New Year resolutions for the sake of progress and tonight is one such occasion."

At the bar Hetty ordered the drinks and then made a big pretence of trying to find her purse claiming it had a silly habit of slipping to the bottom of her bag. To help find it she removed some of the contents and laid them on the counter. One of the items was the January edition of the Pentrillick Gazette. Her plan worked. It caught the landlord's eye as he placed the drinks on a bar mat.

"Are you from Pentrillick then?"

Hetty smiled sweetly. "Yes, all our little group are. It's a lovely village. Do you know it at all?"

"Never actually been there but it's where one of our regulars used to live. Don't know whether you knew him or not but his name was Nigel Taylor."

Hetty couldn't believe her luck. "Oh, yes, the poor man who died from a heart attack just before Christmas. I didn't know him but I believe he was only fifty three. Very sad."

"That's right, he was just fifty three. Same age as me."

As Hetty paid for the drinks the man alone who had earlier been reading his newspaper approached the bar with an empty pint glass.

"Don, these ladies are from Pentrillick," the landlord said.

"Really, did you know Nigel by any chance?"

Hetty shook her head. "No, I was just saying that to your landlord here. Did you?"

"Yes, I did. He and I were great mates. We used to play dominoes together. I really miss him." He spoke with sadness.

"Oh, I am sorry. It's hard to lose a friend."

"It is, and for a few seconds, lady, you raised my hopes. I thought as you came from Pentrillick you might have known him and could have told me what had been troubling him. It really bothers me that I can't find out as I'm sure whatever it was might have been the cause of his heart attack."

Hetty eyes flashed. "Something was troubling him?"

"Yes, he was alright until around last September October time. After that he seemed a bit distant. You know, he kept looking over his shoulders and seemed to be on edge. I asked him what was wrong and he said that it was nothing and it must be my imagination. But it wasn't and now we hear his landlady was murdered in the house he lived in. My instincts tell me something's not right. I just hope he hadn't done summat really bad."

The pub landlord agreed. "Yes, since he's been gone, Don and me have often chatted about Nigel's change of mood but for all that we're none the wiser."

"The police were here yesterday asking about him," said Don, "They didn't say why but they wanted to know who he mixed with and stuff like that. I told them all I knew which wasn't much I must admit. They asked if he drove here and I said no, he came in on an early bus and went back on the last one. Dunno whether they thought he might have been drinking and driving but whatever I assured them he never did."

"Really, that's interesting," Hetty put the remaining items she'd spread on the bar back into her handbag, "Do you know what line of work he was in?"

Don chuckled. "Ah, we do that. He was a computer wizard, wasn't he, Reg? Sometimes he got chatting about technology and stuff and we hadn't a clue what he was on about but we didn't like to let on that we were ignoramuses."

Reg nodded. "You're right, we didn't understand a word of it. It was gobbledygook to the likes of us."

Don glanced towards the table where he had been sitting. "And then on top of losing Nigel I almost lost another mate. Well, he wasn't a mate he was just someone I met in here. You know the young reporter chap they mentioned on the telly. He and I joined forces for the quiz that Sunday. We won as well and then the poor lad got run down after he left here. I do hope he pulls through. He was such a nice lad."

Hetty's jaw dropped. "You met Craig Western?" she squeaked.

"Yes, only briefly though."

"You've no idea what happened to him, I suppose?"

Don shook his head sorrowfully. "Sadly not. After he'd gone I had another pint. It wasn't until we heard all the commotion that we knew something had happened and even then we didn't know it was Craig. Of course that brought the cops in here as well but none of us were able to tell them anything about the young man as we'd never clapped eyes on him before that weekend. I just knew his Christian name. Never even thought to ask what he did because our main focus was the quiz."

The brief conversation was brought to an end when a young couple walked in and approached the bar. Hetty smiled sweetly, picked up the drinks, nodded to the two men and returned to the table in the corner with her head spinning.

Over their drinks Hetty quietly repeated what had been said at the bar hoping she was not overheard. They all then sat in silence and mulled over her words. As Debbie finished her wine she looked at her watch. "If we go now we can catch the next bus which leaves in twenty minutes."

"I suggest we do that then," said Lottie, "as there's nothing more to be gained by staying."

Kitty drank the last of her tonic water. "I agree and we'll be able to talk freely as we walk to the bus station."

The ladies all rose, put on their coats, carried their empty glasses to the bar and said goodnight to the landlord. When she caught his eye, Hetty waved to Don. He waved back and said, "Let me know if you hear anything."

Hetty smiled and raised her thumb.

On their way out, they also said goodbye to Tony and Gus.

"Well, all in all I think that was quite a productive evening," said Hetty, as they stepped onto the pavement.

Debbie agreed. "And I must admit I really enjoyed it despite our initial apprehension."

"So what shall we do now we've found out a bit more?" said Kitty.

Lottie took her gloves from her pocket. "I suggest we sleep on information received and then have a meeting tomorrow morning."

They all agreed to meet at Primrose Cottage at eleven o'clock.

Chapter Seventeen

On Thursday morning, Kitty and Debbie arrived at Primrose Cottage within minutes of one another. Debbie carried a ginger cake she had made straight after breakfast and Kitty brought homemade coconut biscuits.

"Well done, ladies," said Lottie, as she was shown the treats. "Hetty and I had intended to do some baking this morning ourselves but we never got round to it."

"That's because we haven't stopped nattering," laughed Hetty.

"I'm not surprised. After all there is much to discuss after last night's adventure." Debbie handed her cake to Hetty who took it into the kitchen.

When coffee was made and the cake was cut and placed in slices on a plate along with the biscuits, the ladies sat around the fire in the sitting room.

Hetty had an open note pad on the arm of her chair. "Right, we've all had time to mull over last night's discoveries, so what are your thoughts?"

Debbie put down her coffee mug and took a biscuit. "You'll probably think me mad but I reckon Nigel Taylor was murdered and the person who did it killed Vivien too and probably even ran Craig Western down."

Lottie gasped. "Wow! That's a bit extreme, Debbie. But if you're right, what on earth can have been the motive?"

"It has to be the fifty thousand pounds," reasoned Debbie, "there's something not right about it. I mean, if it was all legit and above board, why was it hidden and in a vacuum cleaner of all places? What's more I think the police think there's a connection as well as me. After all we now know they went to the Nag's Head on Tuesday asking about Nigel and his associates and before that they questioned the pub's drinkers about Craig's hit and run. Although I have to admit that the Craig visit would have been because he was on his way back from there when he was hit."

Hetty drummed her fingers on the blank page of the notebook. "What do you think, Kitty?"

"There's no question in my mind that the money was the reason Vivien died but I'm not so sure about Nigel. I mean, the pathologist said it was a heart attack so there's no doubt about that and I just can't see that him being worried about something would have been enough to have brought on a heart attack and even if that was the case it wouldn't be murder, would it?"

"I don't know," said Hetty, "they do say that stress kills so that could be the case with Nigel. And remember, according to Don in the Nag's Head, Nigel was on edge all the time and something seemed to be troubling him, but I agree, stressing him out and bringing on a heart attack surely can't be classed as murder."

"And it could never be classed as premeditated," added Lottie, emphatically.

"Maybe not murder then but according to Don thingy he kept looking over his shoulder," Debbie reminded them, "so maybe someone knew about the money and Nigel felt he was being watched. Or maybe he just had a guilty conscience and was afraid of having his collar fingered."

"So are you implying that he got the money illegally?" Hetty asked.

Debbie nodded. "Yes, something like that."

"In which case perhaps he was a drug dealer," said Kitty, "There's a lot of it about and if he was clever with computers and things like that he could well have been buying dodgy stuff on the dark web."

"Hmm, good point," agreed Debbie, "so what do we know about the dark web?"

Hetty looked at the ladies present. All had blank expressions.

"Perhaps we could Google it," Lottie suggested.

Debbie shook her head. "I don't think that's a good idea because if we did we might get a visit from the police thinking we were trying to access it."

Kitty shuddered. "Best to put that idea to bed then." The agreement was unanimous.

"This is so frustrating." Hetty took another piece of cake and a biscuit as a consolation. The other three ladies equally frustrated did likewise.

"If only we'd known Nigel," said Lottie, "then it'd be easier to try and fathom him out."

"Same goes for Vivien," said Kitty. "None of us knew her either."

"Lottie and I did meet Craig though. So that's one out of the three."

"Yes, but then where does the attempted murder of Craig fit in?" said Debbie, "Did he know something and someone wanted to silence him permanently? It must be something like that."

Hetty's mouth turned upside down. "Goodness only knows. I've given it a lot of thought but I must admit I'm none the wiser."

"But it's probable that whoever the driver was might not have known him anyway. We've already considered the possibility that he might have been drunk or drugged and so couldn't risk stopping," Lottie reminded them,"

"And we mustn't forget that Pickle saw flashing lights in number thirteen a few days before Graham gave everything away," said Kitty, "meaning someone was still looking for something even then and it wasn't the money because everyone knew by then that it had been found."

"It wasn't Nigel's phone and laptop either," said Debbie, "because they were taken on the night Vivien was killed."

"Oh dear, questions, questions, questions," Hetty grumbled, "The more we find out the less we know."

"I suggest we go to the pub tonight for inspiration," enthused Debbie, "I find wine makes my thoughts flow more freely and at the moment I can't see the wood for the trees."

Kitty groaned. "I'd have to be on lemonade if we did. I had a throbbing head this morning."

"But you only had two glasses of wine," chuckled Hetty.

"Yes, and as I said last night that's twice what I would normally have."

"We can't go anyway," said Lottie, "at least Het can't because she's gadding off out tonight."

Debbie licked her sticky fingers. "You are? So where are you gadding off to?"

Hetty shrugged her shoulders. "I don't actually know."

"You don't know!" Debbie was nonplussed.

"She's off out with lover boy." It was not possible to tell whether Lottie was amused or annoyed.

Kitty gasped. "You mean that handsome Charles chap?"

Hetty felt herself blush. "Don't get excited. We're just going out for a meal to catch up with old times."

"But in the old times you were a unit," reasoned Debbie.

Hetty refused to rise to the bait.

"Anyway," said Kitty, "if Hetty's out tonight I suggest we meet in the Crown and Anchor tomorrow at seven to make sure we get our table by the fire."

Debbie rubbed her hands together. "Yes, and then as well as furthering our investigations, Hetty can fill us in with the details of tonight's tête-à-tête."

On Thursday evening at half past seven precisely, Charles Rowlett parked his car on the grass verge opposite Primrose Cottage. From the passenger seat he picked up a bouquet of red roses. When he rang the doorbell, Hetty answered. He kissed her on the cheek and handed her the flowers.

"You're looking beautiful, Henrietta, if I may be permitted to say so."

"Thank you, Charles. I'll just pop these in water and then I'll be ready to go." Hetty closed the door after he stepped into the hallway.

"I'll do them if you like, Het, if you want to get off." Lottie finished the row she was knitting and placed the ends of the needles into her ball of wool.

"Are you sure you don't mind?"

"Of course not. I like arranging flowers and it's not something we do much of in January."

Hetty handed the flowers to her sister. "Then thank you and we'll be off."

Lottie watched from the light of their outside lamp as they walked out in the lane and climbed into Charles' car; as it drove away she realised it must be the flashy top of the range vehicle that Tommy had seen in the Crown and Anchor's car park. Lottie closed the door, took the flowers into the kitchen and arranged them artistically in Hetty's favourite lead crystal vase. Once done, she placed the flowers on the table in the sitting room alongside Debbie's daffodils where they would benefit from the daylight.

The house felt quiet without her sister; Albert was fast asleep in his basket and the only sound was the wind eerily whistling down the chimney. For a while she watched the flickering flames in the fire, mesmerised by their ever changing patterns, and then feeling lonely, she switched on the television and half-heartedly watched a cookery programme. Seeing food prepared made her hungry and so she turned off the television and went into the kitchen where she made herself a sandwich and took the last slice of Debbie's ginger cake. As she ate it she wondered where Hetty and Charles had gone for their meal and if their reunion was likely to become serious. Lottie shuddered. If it did, what would become of her? To push the negative thoughts from her mind, she turned the television back on and watched a documentary programme about chimpanzees.

At ten o'clock she heard a car pull up outside. Two doors opened and then closed followed by the sound of a key in the lock. Lottie looked towards the sitting room door and Hetty walked in followed by Charles.

"Sit down, Charles, while I make coffee." Hetty smiled at her sister, "Would you like one, Lottie?"

Lottie felt she ought to make herself scarce. "Well actually I was just thinking of going to bed." However, the expression on her sister's face caused her to change her mind, "but I had a sandwich earlier and the ham seemed a little salty so a coffee would be lovely, thank you."

Hetty winked as she left the room for the kitchen.

"So, Charles, did you have a nice meal?" Lottie forced herself to be sociable for her sister's sake.

"Yes, thank you, Charlotte. The landlord of the Crown and Anchor recommended a restaurant where he and his wife go on their day off and it was very nice."

"Lovely," Lottie felt impish, "So tell me, Charles, do you ever see anything of Peggy these days?"

"Well, funnily enough, yes. She'd moved to Surrey four or five years ago and soon after she settled in she looked me up."

"That's sweet but how did she know where to find you?"

"I suppose she must have heard on the grapevine that I had moved to London to further my career, and Googling my name, would of course, have brought up the dental practice in which I was a partner until I retired."

"Really! And so did you meet her then?"

"Yes, we met up for a drink one evening to catch up with old times. It was rather pleasant."

"So did she ever marry?"

Charles shook his head. "No, I don't think Peggy was really the marrying kind."

Lottie leaned forwards. "Does she still have crooked overlapping teeth?"

"No, she has beautiful teeth now. Gleaming white and as straight as a die."

"Really! She must have found a damn good dentist then."

Charles stroked his chin which showed off his perfectly manicured nails. "Yes she did but it wasn't me. Her teeth are now false, Charlotte. Every one of them and what a difference it makes. Her face despite a few lines is very attractive now."

"Oh dear. False teeth and she's not yet turned seventy. Hetty still has all her own teeth."

"So I noticed, but then Henrietta was blessed with a fine set of teeth. Quite a contrast to Peggy. Of course I always notice teeth; they make such a huge contribution to one's looks, don't you think?"

"Are you warm enough? If not I'll make the fire up." Lottie, conscious that one of her top teeth was missing and its gap was clearly visible when she spoke, was keen to steer the conversation away from teeth.

"I'm fine, thank you," he glanced around the room, "You have a very nice house here, Charlotte."

"Thank you, we like it."

"You must come up and see it in daylight," Hetty said as she entered the room with three mugs of coffee, "we have a lovely view of the village and the sea beyond."

Charles took the proffered mug. "Is that an invitation?"

Hetty sat down. "Of course. We're proud of our home and always happy to show people around."

"In which case I shall call on you one morning in the foreseeable future."

"Yes, please do. We're in most days, especially this time of the year and often don't go out until the evening. Apart from walking Albert, that is."

"Ah yes, your social life centres around bingo, quiz nights, the drama group and gardening club meetings. Except you're not taking part in this year's drama group production and the gardening club is not meeting this month."

Hetty laughed. "You remembered."

"I listen to your every word, Henrietta."

"I'm flattered."

Lottie pulled a face.

After the coffee was drunk, Charles stood up. "Well, thank you very much for a lovely evening, Henrietta, but I must leave you ladies now as I'm sure you'll be wanting to get your beauty sleep," He looked at Lottie as he spoke.

Hetty saw him to the door and waved him off.

"Humph, beauty sleep indeed," scoffed Lottie as her sister returned to the room.

Hetty smiled. "He knows you don't like him and for that reason he seems to enjoy winding you up."

"It's not that I don't like him it's just that...um, well I don't trust him. He hurt you once and I don't want him to do the same again."

Hetty kissed Lottie's cheek. "We just went out for a meal, that's all. Two old friends catching up on old times. Honestly, there's nothing to worry about and he'll not break my heart again. I promise."

Chapter Eighteen

On Friday afternoon, Norman arrived home from work earlier than usual having finished painting the last room of the Spencers' house in Hawthorn Road. As he unlocked the door of 'Wits' End' and stepped inside he instinctively felt that something was amiss. He wandered around the rooms; everything seemed normal but nevertheless he was not at ease. His sixth sense told him that someone had been inside the house but he couldn't say why. Nor could he see whether things were as he left them in the morning because when he had gone off to work Jackie was still at home as she wasn't due in at work until half past eleven for the lunchtime opening at the Crown and Anchor. Still feeling uneasy he reached for the kettle to make a cup of tea. As he turned to the cupboard where the mugs were kept he saw from the corner of his eye that the bottom drawer handle had come off and was lying on the floor. As he bent to pick it up, the front door opened. Jackie was home.

"Why the glum face, Norm?" She took off her coat and hung it on a peg on the back of the door.

"Did you break this handle off?" He pointed to the drawer and held up the handle.

"No, it was alright last time I saw it. Where was it then?"

"On the floor."

"That's odd. I don't think it was even loose, was it? Anyway, why would it have come off? That drawer's empty."

"Exactly, and it's strange because as soon as I walked through the door I felt someone had been in here but the feeling's worn off now you're home."

Jackie glanced at Norman's fluffy tabby cat curled up in his basket. "Pity you can't talk, Muffins, because if someone has been in here then you must have seen him."

The cat raised its head a little and opened one eye.

"Humph, and if someone had broken in he'd no doubt have rubbed himself around the intruder's legs and turned on the charm instead of hissing with his back arched in order to see him off. Wouldn't you, Muffins?"

On hearing his name for the second time the cat assumed it was time to be fed and so stepped from his basket, stretched and walked to Norman who bent down to stroke his old friend.

"He's got you well and truly under his paw," Jackie removed her boots and reached beneath the kitchen table for her slippers. "So, how come you're back already, Norm?"

"I've finished the Hawthorn Road job so now Graham Spencer can tell the estate agents to put a board up and get things moving."

"Oh yeah of course, I remember you said last night that there wasn't much more to do."

"Even less than I thought and I had it all done by two. Anyway, fancy a cup of tea? I was just about to make one when I spotted the handle on the floor."

"Yes, please, but I must pop to the loo first. I had a pint of lager when I finished work."

"Drinking at lunch time. That's not like you."

"Yeah, I didn't intend to but it was bought for me by an admirer."

"An admirer."

"Don't sound so surprised," Jackie laughed, "Actually it was someone I helped out the other day. An elderly woman was in the shop and found she'd left her purse at home so I loaned her a tenner. She came in today to pay me back and bought me a drink at the same time." Jackie went off to the smallest room but when she returned to the kitchen she seemed perplexed. "You know what you said about it felt like someone had been in here?" Norman nodded, "Well, I reckon you're right. The towel in the downstairs loo was on the floor and so was my hair gel and comb."

"Really!" Norman took a sip of his tea, "When I've drunk this I'm going to have a look round upstairs and check my room. Something's not right."

Jackie sat down. "Yeah, I think I'll do the same."

At first glance Jackie thought everything in her room seemed as she had left it but then she noticed a corner of fabric poking out from the drawer containing her spare bedding. She opened it up. The bedding was not as neat as she kept it. She tried the other drawers. They too had been gone through. She scratched her head, puzzled, for nothing appeared to be missing.

Likewise along the landing Norman found most things as he had left them. It wasn't possible to say if anyone had been through his drawers as they weren't tidy in the first place but someone had been through the shelf where he kept his books. Unlike his clothes which he just threw in the drawers, his kept his books in alphabetical order. And he knew they were in order because he had meticulously gone through them when Sid had given him a dozen military thrillers from the house in Hawthorn Road.

"Right," said Jackie, when they were both back downstairs, "I think we're both in agreement that someone has been in here today. The question is why if nothing was taken?"

"The question is also how? I mean how did someone get in? The back and front doors were both locked and we're the only ones with keys."

Jackie shuddered. "I hadn't thought of that."

"I mean, it's January for goodness sake so the windows are all closed."

Jackie jumped up. "The one in the downstairs loo is always slightly open and remember I found the towel, my hair gel and my comb on the floor in there so they could have been knocked down when someone climbed in through the window because my comb and gel were on the sill."

Jackie went down the hallway and Norman followed. Both stood in the doorway of the downstairs toilet.

Norman looked at the window and then patted his stomach. "No-one could have got through there."

"I could," said Jackie, "at least I could if there was something to stand on outside."

Instinctively they both dashed out the back door and round to the side of the house. Beneath the small frosted window were a few metal bottle tops. Norman walked towards the fence and picked up one of the recycling boxes in a corner by their shed. "Someone must have tipped the stuff out from here and then used it to stand on."

"Good thinking, and in their haste to put the stuff back and get away, they didn't notice the bottle tops which must have been stuck in the gunk in the bottom of the box." Jackie took the box from Norman, placed it beneath the window then stood on it. It was the perfect height for her to climb through the window. Pleased with their detective work, they went back inside the house.

"Well that's one part of the mystery solved," said Norman, "now we just need to find out who it was and what on earth they were looking for."

On Friday evening, Norman went for a pint with Lottie's son, Bill who lived in the Old Bakehouse along the main street. Bill and Norman had been friends since 2018 when Norman delved into his past and established that the Old Bakehouse was where he had lived back in the late fifties until he was two years old.

Sitting on barstools with pints in hand, Norman told Bill about the mystery break-in. Tess who was working behind the bar heard what was said.

"Forgive me for eavesdropping but what you've told Bill is interesting, Norman, because over the past few days I've heard several people say the same thing. You know, someone's been in their houses and had a poke around but nothing appears to have been taken."

Bill chuckled. "Pentrillick must have a very fussy thief then if he can't find anything to his liking."

Tess took two wine glasses from a shelf. "That's what everyone's saying. We're all nonplussed," She left to pour wine for a customer at the other end of the bar.

Norman looked at Bill. "You've not had anyone nosing around your place then?"

"No but then I suppose a thief couldn't be sure when there would be no-one home. Sandra's hours at the care home are irregular and my shifts at the supermarket vary from week to week and then of course the twins are home after school and sometimes during the day as well if they've no lessons."

"No lessons?"

"They're doing their A-levels so have several free periods for studying. Sometimes they use them to study at school and other times they come home early or go in late."

"I see and you just made a good point. Someone must know that I go off painting during the daytime and that Jackie does the lunchtime shift here. I'll have a word with Jay when I next see him and ask if he saw anyone lurking around today."

"I should have a word with Sophie and Ivor as well. I mean they're both away working during the day so they might have had an intruder."

"True, although Ivor's work is irregular too. Paramedics don't work nine 'til five, you know."

"Ah, no of course not. I was forgetting that's what he is. So how do you reckon whoever he was got inside your place?"

"Downstairs loo window without doubt because we always leave it partly open. Whoever he is must be skinny though because there's no way someone built like me could squeeze through that tiny gap."

"Could have been a woman then," reasoned Bill.

"Yeah, Jackie could get through easily. And talking of Jackie, since you have a wife and two teenage daughters, can I ask your advice about something?"

"That sounds sinister, but fire away."

"No, it's nothing sinister. It's just that after Jackie washed her hair this morning she asked me if I thought it'd look better if she did away with her usual spikes and grew it longer. I wasn't sure what to say. I mean, being a crusty old bachelor that's not really something I ever get asked."

Bill chuckled. "So what did you say?"

"I said I liked her spikes but she looked really pretty when she wore the wig on New Year's Eve even though she moaned about it at the time. I would like to have said she'd look more feminine if it was longer but thought that might not go down very well. Although she's not as much of a tomboy as she was when we lived in Dawlish and she doesn't wear studs in all the ear piercings like she used to."

"And what was her response?"

"She said she thought she'd grow it because if she didn't like it she could always get it cut and go back to the spikes. And I said I looked forward to seeing the result."

Bill slapped Norman on the back. "I think your answer was spot on then and very diplomatic if I may say so."

Around the table beside the fire sat four ladies who liked to think of themselves as amateur detectives. And when Lottie went to the bar and saw her son, Bill, she naturally spoke to him and asked after the family. Bill, knowing his mother, his aunt and their friend's predilection for solving crimes told her of the break-in at Norman's house and several others in the village too. Lottie was intrigued and even more so when she learned that nothing was taken. With drinks on a tray she hurried back to the table by the fire to relay the latest piece of information.

"This is starting to make my head hurt," Hetty drank half her glass of wine in one go without even realising she had done so.

"Have you got your notebook with you, Het?" Debbie asked.

"Yes, I always carry it with me because I never know when it might be needed."

"Good, well open it on a clean page and let's write down all the salient facts with asterisks."

Hetty fished out the notebook from her handbag and laid it on the table. After much humming and hawing they had a list.

"Excellent, now read it out, Het," said Debbie.

Hetty cleared her throat. "Right –
  *Nigel Taylor died just before Christmas. Cause of death, a heart attack…or was it?
  *Vacuum cleaner acquired by Lottie and Hetty.
  *Vivien Spencer died. Cause of death, suffocation with a cushion.
  *Nigel Taylor's laptop and phone stolen on the night Vivien was murdered.
  *Dark-coloured, four-wheel drive vehicle seen leaving Hawthorn Road on night of murder.
  *£50,000 discovered in vacuum cleaner…why was it there?
  *Craig Western called at Primrose Cottage for story of said vacuum cleaner.

*Craig Western knocked down by a car in Wesley Road, Penzance...why and by whom?
*Pickle saw flashing lights at house in Hawthorn Rd...who was that?
*Graham Spencer gave contents of 13, Hawthorn Rd away.
*Visit to the Nag's Head revealed Nigel Taylor was troubled by something...but what?
*Visit to the Nag's Head revealed Craig and Don had entered quiz together on the night Craig was knocked down.
*Learn police had been to the Nag's Head and asked questions about Nigel.
*Discover break-ins at certain homes in the village during which nothing was taken...but why?"

"I see," said Debbie, "so where does that leave us?"
Hetty groaned. "In need of another drink, I think."

Chapter Nineteen

"Oh dear," sighed Lottie, as she joined Hetty in the kitchen of Primrose Cottage for breakfast on Saturday morning, "February the first already. This year's flying by as fast as last year although Christmas seems forever ago."

Hetty spread marmalade thickly on her second slice of toast. "I agree, and the year before and the year before that flew by too. In fact every year since I've retired seems to have gone much faster than the years did when we were young."

"And before the month is out, we'll have had another birthday, Het. It's bonkers to think that we'll soon be sixty-eight. I remember our eighth birthday as though it was yesterday." Lottie checked the water level and then switched on the kettle.

"Me too. That was the year Mum and Dad splashed out and bought us both bikes because they'd had a small win on the Football Pools."

"And then we took our Cycling Proficiency Test at school and passed with flying colours. I still have my badge somewhere along with my Prefect's badge from big school."

Hetty put the lid back on the marmalade. "You know what, Lottie, I think we ought to get ourselves a bike each. It'd be good exercise and fun whizzing down Long Lane without pedalling."

"But hard work coming back up."

"Hmm, good point. Perhaps we'll stick to walking."

On hearing mention of his favourite pastime, Albert appeared in the doorway, tail wagging.

"You don't miss a trick, do you flappy ears?" Hetty leaned over and stroked the small dog's head, "Okay, it's a lovely day so we'll go out as soon as I've finished breakfast which won't be long because it's Auntie Lottie's turn to wash up."

Later in the morning, shortly after Kitty had put in an appearance, Debbie arrived at Primrose Cottage by car. En route she had picked up Betsy Triggs from Sunnyside, her home along the main street in the village. Betsy was an elderly widow who in her younger days was in the WRAF where she worked in Intelligence. For this reason it was deemed she might be able to shed some light on the mysteries puzzling not only Lottie, Hetty, Debbie and Kitty, but the police force as well.

Hetty, having seen the pair step from the car, rushed to the front door to let them in. "Welcome to our humble abode," She stretched out her hand to help Betsy over the threshold. "So glad you could make it."

"Thank you for inviting me. I must admit it's a treat to get out. January and February aren't my favourite months. Having said that, I've had quite a bit of companionship lately. The actor lads next door, you know, Gerald and Quincey, they pop in to make sure I'm okay most days and have done ever since they saw me struggling to put out my rubbish bag one wet and very windy morning."

Hetty closed the door. "That's good: I'm glad you've met them after your initial scare."

"I should imagine they're quite good company," said Debbie, "I've heard several people say they both have a great sense of humour and are master raconteurs."

"That's so true and they're good listeners too. The other day I was telling them about the mysterious death of Vivien Spencer. They were fascinated and are as keen to know who did it as you are. I'm looking forward to hearing what you've so far discovered."

Hetty led Betsy into the sitting room and guided her to the armchair beside the fire.

"Lovely sight, you can't beat the look of a fire on a cold winter's day although it's quite pleasant out this morning and a real treat to see the sun shining."

"It is pleasant and I couldn't agree more about a fires," said Lottie. When all were seated, she asked if everyone wanted coffee. They did and as she turned to leave the room for the kitchen, she heard an engine stop outside. "Another car?" She went to the window where the roof of a vehicle was visible over the garden wall as it backed onto the grass verge opposite their house. When the driver stepped out, she chuckled. "Oh, I say. Straighten your hair, Het. Lover boy's here."

"Oh no. We don't want him here while we're discussing things. He'll think us bonkers." Hetty was flustered.

"Don't worry, it's not a problem," said Debbie, "We'll just pretend we've assembled for coffee and a chat and we can discuss the important stuff when he's gone."

"Good thinking," chuckled Lottie, "if we chat about women's things he might get bored and leave early."

Hetty answered the door after Charles had knocked. He handed her another bouquet of flowers.

"Oh, Charles, you shouldn't have."

He kissed her cheek. "Why not. It isn't often one has the opportunity to call at the home of a very dear friend."

Hetty closed the door. "I hope you don't mind but we have a few of our friends here this morning. They often call for a natter over coffee."

"Not at all, I should be delighted to meet them. Any friend of yours Henrietta is a friend of mine."

She led him into the sitting room. "Now you've already met Debbie and Kitty, but have yet to meet Betsy."

Charles took Betsy's hand and brushed it with a kiss. "Delighted to make your acquaintance, dear lady."

"Likewise," Betsy felt flattered, "and how nice to meet a gentleman."

"Please make yourself comfortable, Charles, while we make coffee for you all." Hetty headed towards the kitchen where Lottie already had the kettle on.

"I'll help as well, it'll save them both making too many trips." Debbie sprang from her chair and dashed from the room leaving Kitty and Betsy to entertain Charles.

The gathering made small talk as they drank coffee and ate chocolates from a box Debbie had brought along; one of the many she had received for Christmas. The chat was not exciting because the ladies were careful to avoid mention of the recent happenings in the village. The weather was a popular topic and Charles was told how the village would soon be preparing for the second Pentrillick in Bloom competition along with other delights of village life.

"And now," said Charles, rising, as they all finished their coffee, "would you care to show me around your delightful home, Henrietta? I'll not have another chance as sadly I return to London this evening."

"Oh, so soon," Hetty sprang to her feet.

"Regrettably, yes."

"Come on then. I'll take you on a grand tour."

Charles closed the door behind him after following Hetty from the room.

"So what do you think of him, Betsy?" Debbie whispered.

"I think he's charming although he seems a little nervous and I noticed he seldom takes his eyes off Hetty. I get the impression he's quite taken with her."

"That's what bothers me. I can't bear to see her hurt again." Lottie's voice quivered with emotion.

"How long is it since they were together?"

147

"Forty-four years."

"Good grief that is a long time ago."

"I wouldn't worry, Lottie," reassured Debbie, "Hetty's got a mind of her own and she's very strong willed. I'm sure she'll not do anything rash and he's going home today anyway."

When the tour ended, Charles and Hetty returned to the sitting room where Charles addressed Lottie, "My dear, Charlotte, you and your lovely sister have a beautiful home. I feel quite envious. I live in a flat, you see. A luxury flat albeit. But my outlook is of buildings and cannot compare with the vista you have here both back and front."

"Thank you, Charles. Hetty and I share your enthusiasm."

"And now I must take my leave of you," he bowed to the ladies, "Thank you for your hospitality."

He left the room and Hetty followed. On the doorstep he took her hands in his. "I hope to see you again one day."

Hetty felt her knees weaken. "That would be nice."

He kissed her hands and looked into her eyes, "Au revoir, my lovely." He then walked across the road to his car and climbed into the driver's seat. As he started the engine he waved, oblivious of the tears welling in Hetty's eyes as she thought of what might have been.

Meanwhile in the sitting room, Charles' departure was watched by four sets of inquisitive eyes.

"That's the posh car Tommy pointed out to me in the pub car park," said Kitty. "He reckons it's new and would have cost a fortune."

"Well, I should imagine there's a lot of money to be made in dentistry," reasoned Debbie, "especially in London and he was a partner before he retired, wasn't he?"

Lottie nodded. "Yes he was. He was also an only child and no doubt inherited his parents' farm on their demise, so that would have boosted his bank balance considerably."

Chapter Twenty

On Sunday evening, the Crown and Anchor was busy again for quiz night.

"I can't believe this is the fourth one already," said Debbie.

Hetty tutted. "It is and we've not been one of the top three winning teams once."

"We need someone with brains to help us. Who can we nab?"

"But we can't have more than six," said Kitty.

"I know but there are only us four this week because Sandra's working and Bill's making her a curry for when she finishes at nine and so they won't be joining us."

Kitty frowned. "Oh dear, we're doomed then."

Debbie nodded towards the bar where the two actors sat on stools. "I wonder if they'd like to join us. I mean, if they did they'd know all the show biz type stuff and other things young people are familiar with like contemporary music."

"Good point and they're on their own so might like to play. So which of you ladies is going to ask them?" Hetty hoped to see a volunteer but it was clear no-one relished the task.

Debbie looked from one face to another. "So how can we decide?"

"We'll draw for it," said Lottie, "let's each put our name in a hat and then ask someone at random to take one out."

Kitty nodded. "Ideal solution."

Hetty shook her head. "But we don't have a hat."

They looked around for something suitable but nothing sprang to mind.

"Have to be this then," Lottie removed one of her ankle boots, "Get your notepad out, Het, tear off a page and write down our names."

When the folded papers of names were inside Lottie's boot, she hopped over to the next table, asked Sid to remove a piece of paper and read the name on it. All eyes in the immediate vicinity watched, intrigued by the happening.

"It's your name," Sid held the piece of paper up, "Look it says Lottie."

"Damn," she pulled out the other three names from her boot, "Thanks, Sid."

"My pleasure but what's this about?"

"Nothing much, it's just I now have to ask the two actor chaps if they'd join our quiz team, that's all."

"That's no problem then. Just flutter your eyelashes."

"Cheeky!" Lottie slipped her boot back on.

To Lottie's relief, the two young actors, having seen and heard the impromptu draw, said they'd be delighted to join the ladies and so they all made room around the table for them to sit. Their addition proved a success and the team came a close second.

"When we popped in to see Betsy the other day she told us about the drama group here in the village and how she wished she was thirty years younger so she could join. Are any of you members?" Quincey asked as they all had a celebratory drink.

"All of us," said Lottie, "but apart from Het we all work backstage. You know, front of house, costumes, refreshments and stuff like that."

"Really, so you've done a bit of acting, Hetty. Are you in this year's production?"

"No, no, I've not been in a play since the one your landlord, Brett wrote. I was the cook and thoroughly enjoyed it. Amateur dramatics is great fun because we don't have the stress that I should imagine you professionals do."

Gerald leaned back in his seat. "Yes, theatre can be stressful, TV too but at least with the latter if you get it wrong you can do it again."

"So what have you lads been doing with yourselves during your stay?" Debbie asked, "I mean this time of the year isn't beach weather. Having said that, I like to see the sea when it's rough. It sounds great too."

"Ah, we agree with you there," said Quincey, "and at Sea View we can watch it without leaving the house, especially from upstairs which is brilliant."

"But to answer your question, we've actually been painting," said Gerald.

"Really! So you're artists then as well as actors," Lottie was impressed.

Quincey crossed his legs and noticed several cat hairs on his trousers; he removed them meticulously one by one. "Only in our dreams" he chuckled, "The painting we've done is with emulsion. That was the agreement with Brett. We could stay in the cottage for as long as we wanted rent free but he asked us to paint the kitchen and bathroom walls because he knew they were getting a bit shabby."

"And we actually enjoyed it," said Gerald, "it's quite therapeutic and we made a reasonably good job, didn't we, Quince?"

"I think so."

"Are you alright, Het?" Kitty saw that Hetty had gone very quiet.

"What? Oh, yes, yes I'm fine."

"You were miles away just then."

"Yes, well, I was just thinking of something."

Kitty, knowing that Charles had returned home assumed it was probably him occupying her friend's thoughts and so said no more.

The ladies left the Crown and Anchor shortly after last orders were rung. They thanked the young actors for coming to their rescue and then after saying goodbye to Debbie at the foot of Long Lane, the ladies who lived in Blackberry Way made their way up the hill towards home. Kitty and Lottie chatted about the quiz, the actors and the evening in general but Hetty still seemed rather quiet.

"Okay," said Lottie, at last, "What's bothering you, Het? You've been quiet ever since we finished the quiz and you had plenty to say before that."

Hetty frowned. "Yes, you're quite right, something is bothering me but because I can't fathom out what, I can't tell you what it is."

"Give us a clue," said Kitty, "We might be able to help."

"It's the actor lads. I don't whether or not you noticed but while you were all talking about rough seas and painting the kitchen and bathroom at Sea View, Quincey plucked some cat hairs from his trouser legs. Something at the back of my mind is telling me that's significant but I can't think what or why."

"Neither can I," chuckled Kitty, "it's hardly an earth shattering act."

"And they were probably dog hairs anyway," said Lottie, "Not that I can see any significance but there were several dogs in the pub tonight."

Unable to see why Hetty was in thought mode, Kitty and Lottie continued their chat.

"I see young Jackie has changed her hairstyle," said Kitty, "I thought it looked so much nicer that those silly spikes."

"Yes, and according to Bill she's going to grow it a bit longer. I think it'll suit her because she looked really pretty on New Year's Eve when she was Alice in Wonderland and wore that blonde wig."

"Jackie," whispered Hetty, "That's it. Jackie and Norman are convinced that someone broke into their place on Friday and according to Norman who was chatting with Bill on Friday night, he and Jackie reckon Muffins would have made a fuss of the intruder rather than see him off. Meaning, whoever the intruder was would most likely have got cat hairs on his trousers because Muffins is a very fluffy cat."

Lottie slowed her pace. "Surely you're not suggesting Quincey broke into Norman's house, Het. That's too daft for words."

Hetty was obstinate. "Is it? I mean, he's the right size to have got in through the toilet window."

"But why would he have done that?" Kitty asked.

"Why would anyone have done it and not taken anything?" Hetty retorted, "Because that appears to be the case, not only with Norman and Jackie but with several other people too."

"Well I think it's bonkers," snapped Lottie, "besides, I'm sure if Quincey had got cat hairs on his trousers he would have brushed them off when he put them on today. So as far as I'm concerned he must have picked them up tonight from one of the dogs. Probably even Barnaby because I saw him talking to Jay and Polly and petting the young pup before we got them to do the quiz."

"Maybe, but they were on the back of his trousers so if they were already there he might not have seen them until he sat down and crossed his legs. Anyway, it's food for thought and I shall add it to our list of happenings when we get home and then tomorrow I'll ring Debbie and see what she thinks."

On Tuesday afternoon, as Norman stepped from his van after returning home from his latest job, wallpapering a bedroom in St Mary's Avenue, his next-door neighbour, Jay opened his front door and waved to him. "Norman I'm so sorry to ask at such short notice but could either you or Jackie keep an eye on Barnaby from time to time for me this evening. Only for a couple of hours. Someone's interested in my art work wants to meet up with me for dinner and it's an opportunity not to be missed. Normally I take Barnaby with me when I go out if Polly's away but I can't tonight as we're meeting in a posh restaurant."

Norman raised his hands. "Say no more, I'll be more than happy to help. Jackie will be working but only in the kitchen tonight so she should be finished by half nine as it's pretty quiet this time of the year."

Jay heaved a sigh of relief. "Thank you so much, I really appreciate it. I ought to be able to leave him on his own but he gets stressed if he's left for long. I think he must have been pretty badly treated by his previous owners."

"In that case I'll stay with him 'til you get back," Norman took a bag containing his lunchbox from the passenger seat. "So what time will you want me?"

"Half eight. Would that be okay? My dinner date is for nine."

"Sounds fine," he closed the van door, "I'll see you then."

At half past eight, Norman rang the bell at the home of his next-door neighbours. Jay answered promptly; he was dressed smartly and reeked of aftershave. As Norman stepped over the threshold it crossed his mind that the party interested in Jay's art work might well be female and attractive to boot.

"I've fed Barnaby and at the moment he seems quite relaxed so you could well be in for a quiet evening." Jay led Norman into the sitting room where Barnaby lay in his basket. On seeing Norman, the small dog sat up and then left his bed, tail wagging; Norman was the nice man who he sometimes saw in the pub who gave him bits of meat from his pasties and so he deserved a warm welcome.

"Looks like he remembers you," said Jay.

Norman sensed that his neighbour was relieved.

"There's plenty of beer in the fridge if you fancy a drink, Norm, and if you're peckish help yourself to whatever takes your fancy." He stroked Barnaby's head and told him to be good.

"I promise, I'll not be late. Well, no later than half eleven anyway. Probably earlier if it doesn't go well."

After Norman heard Jay's car drive away he went into the kitchen and took a can of beer from the fridge. As he sat on the sofa and switched on the television, Barnaby jumped up beside him and settled with his head on Norman's lap.

"Anything you particularly like to watch?" Norman asked as he flicked through the endless list of television channels.

Barnaby yawned.

"I know how you feel," said Norman. He switched off the television and they both took a nap.

An hour later Norman was woken by a gentle knock on the door. He sprang to his feet and went to answer it. Barnaby followed. On the doorstep stood Jackie. "Do you want some company?" She knelt to make a fuss of the small dog.

"Yes, come in. Busy in the pub tonight?"

"We did a few meals but not many but then it is February and Tuesday's not very busy anyway."

"Was Bill in?"

"I don't think so. His mum and his aunt were. In fact they arrived with Debbie just as I was leaving."

Norman quietly closed the door.

"Hmm, they've got this place nicely furnished," said Jackie, as they went into the sitting room.

"They have but I'm not very keen on Jay's paintings." Norman pointed to a large framed picture at the far end of the room. Guess what that is?"

Jackie tilted her head from one side to the other. "Well the colours look a bit like a sunset or sunrise but I'm not convinced."

Norman clapped his hands. "Well done. You're right. It's the sun setting over the sea."

Jackie sat down. "Hmm, I think prefer Ella's version of a Cornish sunset. In fact Jay ought to take some lessons from her."

"Fancy a beer? I'm having another."

"Yes please."

Norman went into the kitchen and took two cans from the fridge. He handed one to Jackie and opened the other for himself. "So were there any exciting happenings in the pub tonight?"

"No, not in the kitchen and I didn't hear of anything from the bar. The most exciting thing is that Harry's popping home from uni for a couple of days this weekend, so that'll be nice."

"I reckon he'll be popping back to see you," Norman teased. "The two of you seemed to get on really well over the Christmas holiday and on New Year's Eve you were laughing together nonstop."

"That's because he looked ridiculous as the knave of hearts and the tarts on the paper plate attached to his tunic front kept falling off."

Norman smiled recalling the heart-warming atmosphere that evening.

"Anyway," continued Jackie, "we do get on but if you're trying to imply there's more to it than that then you'll be wrong. What's more, I'm older than him and I reckon he's more interested in the young waitresses than the likes of me."

Norman felt a sudden lump in his throat and realised how empty his life would be if she were to find a partner and move away.

Chapter Twenty-One

As usual on Tuesday evening, Hetty and Lottie met up with Debbie in the village hall for a few games of bingo and then afterwards all three went to the Crown and Anchor for a glass or two of wine. As they sat down and Lottie placed the drinks she had bought on the table, Debbie cast her eyes around the bar. "It looks as though Gus and Tony have moved on. I've not seen them for a while now."

"Yes, I dare say they have," agreed Lottie, "Nearly all our daffodils are in bloom now so I suppose commercially there's no market for them."

Debbie leaned over and held her chilled right hand in front of the fire to bring back life into her dead white fingers. "Betsy said that Gerald and Quincey have gone home as well, so it's probably back to locals only now until Easter although I suppose there will be a few extra people around during half term week if the weather's reasonable."

Hetty eyes flashed. "Gerald and Quincey have gone. When did Betsy tell you that?"

"This evening. I meant to tell you but forgot. I was a bit early for bingo and so popped in to see if she was okay and she told me then. I think she was quite sad. They bought her flowers and chocolates before they went and promised they'd see her again soon because they loved the village and would like to think of it as somewhere to escape the pressures of modern day life."

"Does that frown on your face mean you still suspect them of breaking into Norman's place?" Lottie asked disapprovingly.

Hetty's frown deepened but she refrained from answering.

"Actually I can explain the cat hairs," laughed Debbie, "Apparently, Quincey is moggy mad. Betsy told me that because her cat - I can't remember its name - always made a big fuss of him and wouldn't leave him alone. And as the lads called in to see her on the way to the pub on Sunday night that would explain the hairs on his trousers."

Hetty's frown turned into a smile. "I'm so glad to hear that, Debbie, because I liked the lads despite what I said and I suppose I was just grasping at straws because I want to see some progress made in the Hawthorn Road case."

"Don't we all?" Lottie sighed.

Debbie nodded. "Yes, we do and I can see where you were coming from, Het. About the cat hairs I mean."

Hetty leaned one elbow on the table and rested her face in her hand. "I just wish we had some suspects because at present we've none and unless something else happens soon I can't see us getting any more clues."

"Ah, that's something else I meant to tell you," said Debbie, "It's not about clues but it does involve number thirteen. You see, Gideon walked home along Hawthorn Road yesterday and he said the estate agent's board in the front garden has 'under offer' plastered on it."

"Really! That was quick," said Hetty.

Lottie shuddered. "I wonder if the potential purchaser knows of its gruesome history."

"That's just what I said to Gideon."

Hetty leaned back and folded her arms. "I wonder if sellers are compelled to tell buyers of things such as that. I know they have to say if there have been any disputes or problems with neighbours and so forth."

"Good point," said Debbie, "but if they do then the purchaser must be pretty dispassionate."

Lottie shook her head. "I can't believe that one person has died and another has been seriously injured over our vacuum cleaner and as far as we know no-one has been arrested let alone charged. I mean, I know as Het said that we've no suspects but surely the police must have someone in mind."

"Well if they have they won't tell us and with every day that passes the trail gets a little colder."

They left the Crown and Anchor earlier than usual after just one drink for heavy rain was forecast and they wanted to be home before it began. At the bottom of Long Lane, the sisters said goodbye to Debbie who made her way through the village to her home in St Mary's Avenue.

The night was silent as Hetty and Lottie walked up the hill towards Blackberry Way. The bare branches of trees and leafless hedgerows cast eerie shadows in the light from the blurry half-moon. When they reached the top of the hill they stood and looked back over the village where lights in houses glowed and stars twinkled above the sea on the distant horizon.

"Beautiful," whispered Hetty, "that view never ceases to amaze me whatever time of day or night."

"Or season," Lottie added, "It's stunning all year round. Even your Charles gave it the seal of approval."

As they approached Primrose Cottage the first thing they noticed was the outside light which they had left on no longer lit up their front garden.

"Damn," said Hetty, as she fumbled in her handbag for the front door key, "it looks like the bulb's gone. What a nuisance."

"Not to worry, we have several spares."

"Yes, I know but it's a bit awkward to change the bulb because the cover's a tight fit and I broke several nails last time we did it. Still, as they say, worse things happen at sea."

As Hetty found the key, Lottie suddenly took hold of her arm. "Look, Het. I've only just noticed but there's a car parked in the gateway over the road. You can just make out its roof in the dim moonlight."

Hetty frowned. "Who can that belong to then? Every house along here has a driveway so it's unlikely to be someone visiting."

"And it wasn't there when we went out anyway."

As they walked towards the gate to take a closer look at the vehicle they were distracted by a crash from inside their house.

"Oh my god, don't say we have a burglar," squealed Lottie.

"Shush! Well if we have let's creep inside and surprise him."

"What! Are you mad? Remember what happened to Vivien."

"But it can't be the same burglar, can it? I mean whoever that was, was after the fifty grand in the vacuum cleaner and it's common knowledge that the police took that money away after we found it," Hetty nodded towards the door, "No, I reckon the chappie paying us a visit must be the one who breaks into houses and doesn't take anything, and as there are two of us we should easily be able to overpower him. Remember, Norman reckons he's small because he must have got in through their downstairs loo window."

"Maybe, but who's to say there's only one of them in there this time? There could be two or even three."

Hetty looked downcast. "Yes, you could be right, so what shall we do? We can't stand here until they've gone because it's freezing and I need to make sure Albert's alright."

Lottie was puzzled. "I wonder why he's not barking."

Hetty slapped her hand over her mouth. "Oh, please don't say they've hurt him."

Lottie pulled her sister away from the house. "We can't do anything about it now. Come on, Het, let's creep back along the road and then ring the police. The sooner they get here the sooner you'll be able to see Albert."

At that moment they heard a tap as something knocked against the landing window. Quickly they looked up just in time to see a figure leap backwards.

"He saw us," gasped Lottie, "Quick let's make a dash for it."

"But where to?"

"Next door's garden. We'll hide amongst the shrubbery. With any luck he'll think we've run off down the lane."

With haste the sisters ran towards Tuzzy-Muzzy. They quickly opened the gate and slipped in between the dense shrubs. No sooner were they hidden than they heard the front door of their house open and close followed by the thudding of feet running across their driveway and over the road. Angry muffled voices were followed by the slamming of car doors. As the car engine started, the sisters raised their heads and through gaps between the shrubs watched the vehicle drive off with speed, its tyres screeching as it clipped the grass verge on the corner and narrowly missed the overhanging branches of a blackthorn bush as it turned into Long Lane. Hetty gasped. The dark coloured vehicle was four-wheel drive.

"I feel sick," cried Lottie, "that has to be the vehicle that Mrs Rudd saw; the one Vivien's killers made their getaway in."

"I agree but did you see anyone in it?"

"There were definitely two people in the front and I think one was a woman. Either that or it was a man with longish hair. I couldn't see if there was anyone in the back."

"I don't think there was because we only heard two car doors open and close."

Confident that the coast was clear, the sisters emerged from their hiding place and to steady themselves walked arm in arm towards their house.

"If it was a woman," said Hetty, "then I've no idea who she might be."

"But it wouldn't be any different if they were both men, would it, Het? I mean, let's face it, as far as the current goings-on are concerned we've not the slightest idea who is behind any of it."

"No, but I've a sneaky feeling that we're getting warmer."

Satisfied that no-one was around, Hetty phoned the police. After explaining the situation they were told not to go into the house until officers arrived. The sisters were relieved as neither felt brave enough to go inside anyway, although Hetty was desperately concerned as to the reason why Albert had not barked when the intruders were inside the house. Huddled together to keep warm they sat on the doorstep and awaited the arrival of the police, both hoping that no damage had been done to their home and possessions.

Chapter Twenty-Two

It seemed much longer, but fifteen minutes later Hetty and Lottie heard sirens. They leapt to their feet and rushed to the gate. Down in the village, blue lights flashed from two vehicles speeding along the main street. For the police, knowing that Primrose Cottage was where the money had been discovered in the vacuum cleaner and where Craig Western the reporter hurt in a hit and run had visited, considered the call-out to be urgent. For not only was it possible that one of the intruders might still be inside the house but there was every chance that forensic evidence might be found, thus enabling them to nail the elusive persons behind the recent spate of criminal activity.

The two vehicles pulled up in the lane and the sisters both sighed with relief as the car doors were hurriedly opened before even the drivers had switched off the engines. From the car nearest the gate, a man in plain clothes stepped from the passenger seat. The sisters recognised him as Detective Inspector Fox with whom they had had dealings in the past.

"Are either of you ladies hurt?" he asked.

"No, no, we're fine. Cold but fine, thank you," Lottie found it hard to speak as her teeth were chattering.

"And we feel a lot better now that you're here." Hetty held up the front door key. Detective Inspector Fox nodded to one of the other three police officers indicating that he should unlock the door.

"Wait here," the DI commanded.

The police went inside and quickly spread out around the house. A few spots of rain fell and so the sisters not wanting to get wet or miss anything disobeyed and cautiously stepped over the threshold and waited on the doormat. They were relieved to see that the hallway looked much as they had left it. After a few moments the DI said there was no-one in the house and he invited the sisters in but asked them not to touch anything. Hetty part obeyed and pushed the front door shut with her foot to keep out the cold. From the hallway the sisters glanced into the sitting room. That also looked as they had left it except that Albert was not in his basket. From the dining room they heard voices and saw that the officers were all in the one room.

"Have you seen Albert?" Hetty blurted.

"No, there's no-one here," said one of the officers.

"Who's Albert?" the DI asked.

"My dog. A Yorkshire terrier."

One of the officers smiled. "Oh, I see. He's in the kitchen gnawing a big fat juicy bone."

Hetty dashed down the hallway while Lottie peeped into the dining room where books were strewn all over the floor but everything else appeared in situ.

After fussing Albert, Hetty joined everyone else. "It looks like they got in through the back door," she whispered to Lottie, "The key's laying on the doormat so I reckon they reached it through the dog flap."

"Really! Same as at number thirteen then."

"Yes, and we really must get into the habit of taking the key from the lock when we're not here."

The attention of the police was focussed on the dining room as it was the only place where there was evidence of disturbance.

"It looks as though someone was looking for something specific rather than here to steal any of your belongings," said the detective inspector, "Without touching anything can you see if there's anything obvious that's missing?"

Hetty shook her head. "Nothing jumps out at me and I've no idea what whoever might have been after."

"I agree and it looks like only the books appear to have been disturbed." Lottie turned to Hetty, "Is Albert alright?"

"Yes, he obviously didn't bark because the intruders gave him a bone and shut him in the kitchen. Soppy thing. Not much of a guard dog."

"And the intruders clearly knew you had a dog," said the DI, "That's interesting."

Hetty shrugged her shoulders. "Yes, but then nearly everyone in the village knows about Albert so it's no secret. Having said that, Lottie, me and our friends think the people behind all this are not locals."

Detective Inspector Fox raised his eyebrows but refrained from commenting.

"Why do you think the burglar was looking through our books, Inspector?" Lottie asked, "I mean, they're worth next to nothing."

"Clearly he was hoping to find something amongst them but what I've no idea. Are you ladies able to tell me anything of their history? Where you acquired them and so forth?"

"They've come from all sorts of places. Some we've had for donkey's years and others we've bought in the charity shop but most of the ones on the floor that were on that shelf came from number thirteen." Hetty pointed to the empty shelf in the alcove.

"Thirteen! Do you mean as in number thirteen Hawthorn Road?"

"That's right. Zac got them for us at the same time as he got the vacuum cleaner. There were military thrillers as well but Zac didn't think we'd be too keen on them so Sid gave them to Norman because he knows they're his favourite genre."

"Hmm, now that is very interesting," Detective Inspector Fox cast his eyes over the scattered books, "So are you able to tell which are which?"

"That's easy," said Lottie, "the ones by the table legs are from this bookcase by the door and we already had them. The ones on the hearth rug were in the alcove and are from number thirteen."

"And what was on this bookcase?" The DI pointed to the empty shelves of a bookcase in the corner.

"Nothing," said Hetty, "we got that from number thirteen as well but haven't yet got round to putting anything in it yet. Our intention is to fill it with the Hawthorn Road books and then put the ornaments crammed on the piano back on the shelf in the alcove which is where they were before we got the books."

"I see," he frowned, "at least I think I do."

"So what might the intruders have been looking for?" Lottie asked again, "I mean, books are books, aren't they? And as far as we know none are first editions or of any value."

"At the moment I can't answer your question and so I think we'd better try and find out. We'll go through them all, every one, and you ladies can help. Check every page for handwritten words or anything tucked inside. There has to be something for someone to have gone to all this trouble."

The officers put on latex gloves and gave the sisters each a pair to do likewise.

"Forensics are on the way," said the detective inspector, "hopefully they'll be able to get prints or some other incriminating evidence."

One of the officers picked up the Hawthorn Road books from the hearth rug and placed them in six piles on the table ready for inspection. Hetty and Lottie, delighted for the opportunity to assist the police, pulled on their gloves and meticulously went through the pile of books placed in front of them, but after every one had been gone through there was nothing to be found other than the occasional inscription and indications that some were ex-library books.

"Perhaps they found what they were looking for," suggested Lottie, "I mean, we weren't familiar with these Hawthorn Road books so we couldn't say if one or several are missing."

Detective Inspector Fox sat down on one of the dining chairs and scratched his head. "I fear you might be right or it's possible that what we're looking for might be amongst the military books given to whoever you said received them."

"Norman," said Lottie, "Norman Williams. He lives in one of the new houses in Cobblestone Close and I've just remembered his house was broken into recently but nothing appeared to have been taken."

The inspector frowned. "Really? I don't recall being told of any other break-ins in the village."

"That's because they weren't reported. I mean, nothing was taken and some folks even wondered if they'd imagined someone had broken in. After all you can hardly call the police to report nothing stolen. It'd be a waste of time and resources."

"Quite right, but it looks as though the intruders might have targeted houses where they knew items had come from Hawthorn Road."

Lottie gasped. "Yes. Norman said that someone had been through his books because they weren't as he kept them in alphabetical order."

"Hmm, we'd better look into that."

Hetty, who hated things to be untidy, looked at the books still on the floor. "Can I put our books back in the bookcase, Inspector? After all we know they're of no interest because they didn't come from Hawthorn Road."

"Yes, please do. It might help unscramble my mind."

Hetty began to fill the bottom shelf and Lottie helped. The DI suddenly sat forwards. "It's just a thought, but are the books all there? I mean did you put any anywhere else? Perhaps you started to read one by the fire or something like that."

"Yes, they're all here, I put them on the shelf myself and..." Hetty gasped, "No, you're right, yes, there are two more. They're upstairs because I like to read at bedtime. I'm half way through one and the second is ready for when I've finished the first. They're by the same author, you see. David Dodge. I'll go and get them."

Hetty left the room and returned minutes later. The books were hardback, quite old and had dust jackets. She placed them on the table. "This is the one I'm reading, *Plunder of the Sun*, it's very good."

Detective Inspector Fox picked up the book and flicked through its pages. He then removed the dust jacket. There was nothing to be found. He picked up the second and did the same. On the back cover, beneath the dust jacket flap, eleven words were scrawled in spidery handwriting, *Twelve Christmas Songs to make your Party go with a Swing*. He looked at the front cover. The book was, *To Catch a Thief*.

"To catch a thief, I remember that being a film," said Lottie, "It was very good."

"Really? I can't say that I remember it," said Hetty.

"Yes, you must have seen it. It was one of Hitchcock's and starred Cary Grant."

The inspector laid down the book on the table. "Well, never mind about the film. I'm more concerned about the message under the dust cover. Does it mean anything to you ladies?"

Lottie turned towards the rack of CDs and scratched her head. "Hmm, yes I must admit it rings a bell. It sounds like a record title or something like that. In fact, I'm sure I've seen it somewhere and I think one of these CDs might be called whatever Christmas party thingy songs."

"Really! And did they by any chance come from Hawthorn Road as well?" Detective Inspector Fox stood up.

"Some of them," said Hetty, "I brought them back on the day Graham Spencer had his big give away but I've never looked to see what's there. It was Lottie who sorted them and put them in the rack."

Lottie knelt down and ran her gloved fingers over the cases; towards the bottom she found what she was looking for. She pulled out the CD case and handed it to the inspector. He opened it. On the right-hand side was a disc with a garish centre saying, 'Twelve Christmas Songs to make your Party go with a Swing'. On the opposite side unclipped was a disc with no label.

"Looks hopeful," said one of the officers.

"It does. Do you ladies have a laptop handy?" the inspector asked.

"In the other room." Hetty was already walking towards the door. In the sitting room she picked up her laptop from the floor and placed it on the table. She then logged on. Nervously the sisters watched as the inspector inserted the disc. The police officers then gathered in front of the laptop. Hetty and Lottie stepped back not wanting to be in the way.

On the screen a picture came up of three men in masks who appeared in a hurry. Behind them was a well-known jewellers. The second picture was similar and so was the third. On the fourth they were approaching a car. On the fifth they were opening the car doors. On the sixth the driver of the car was clearly visible as his face was not covered.

"Well I never. It looks as though someone took a few pictures of jewellery thieves making their get-away. No doubt the photographer used a mobile phone and then transferred them onto a disc. How very kind of him."

The officer nearest the DI looked and nodded at the screen. "Do you know him, sir? The driver that is?"

"No, but then if I remember correctly that particular robbery took place up country, London somewhere I believe and so he's not on our beat. Anyway, we'll get these printed off and circulated amongst other forces and see if anyone recognises him."

"May we have a look?" Hetty's fingers twitched excitedly.

"Yes, of course," Detective Inspector Fox stood back. Hetty took one look at the screen and then fainted.

Chapter Twenty-Three

Because of their involvement, Detective Inspector Fox felt it was only right that the ladies at Primrose Cottage were given an explanation as to why the money hidden in the vacuum cleaner which found its way into their possession was put there in the first place. Likewise, why the pictures transferred onto a compact disc from a mobile phone were found amongst the CDs they had acquired from the house in Hawthorn Road. Then there was the fact they had been terrified by an attempted robbery and their pet dog Albert had been put at risk. Not only did he feel that the ladies deserved an explanation, he felt that it was his duty to perform the task himself. He asked a member of his staff to make an appointment, as a result he called at Primrose Cottage the following day. The sisters were ready and waiting with a freshly baked cake and a welcoming fire.

After his visit, as pre-arranged, Kitty and Debbie, who knew nothing of the disc or even the break-in at Primrose Cottage, arrived to hear the latest news the sisters claimed to have. With mugs of coffee and a slice each of cake they sat in the sitting room by the fire.

To their surprise it was Lottie who began the explanation. "As you will understand in due course, Het's finding it hard to come to terms with what's happened and so you'll have to put up with me reading this letter." She took an envelope from the table.

"Letter?" said Debbie, "Who from?"

"Yes, a letter and you'll realise who it's from when I begin to read it. You see, as much as Detective Inspector Fox wanted to tell us what had happened of late he knew that he couldn't for legal reasons and so he asked someone who was able to tell us to write a letter to explain. The person in question had already confessed: he is now in police hands up-country and for that reason was happy to comply with the DI's request." Lottie removed a sheet of paper from the envelope.

Debbie frowned. "Right, I see, at least I think I do."

Kitty looked from Lottie to Hetty. "Hmm, same here but I didn't know anyone had been arrested and I can't believe you didn't tell us."

"It only happened yesterday and we didn't tell you because we were asked not to. I'm sorry but you'll soon see why." Lottie cleared her throat and unfolded a sheet of paper covered on both sides in neat handwriting. *"Dear Henrietta and Charlotte,"* she read.

Debbie gasped. She looked at Hetty. "No, it can't be from…"

Hetty nodded. "Yes, it is," she whispered.

"But…"

"Let Lottie continue," said Kitty.

"Thank you," Lottie started again,

Dear Henrietta and Charlotte,

I don't know whether or not you remember but in early September last year there was a robbery at a jewellery shop in West London. Four people were involved although initially the police thought there were only three. As the robbers made off with an extensive collection of jewels, Nigel Taylor, late of Hawthorn Road, was in a café on the opposite side of the road and instinctively he took several pictures on his mobile phone of the get-away. His reason being that it might help the police get a conviction as the driver, needing not to draw attention to himself as he waited in the get-away car, wore no mask. Nigel

172

was in London for a technology exhibition at Olympia and when he went back to his hotel room he looked closely at the pictures he'd taken through his laptop and to his amazement realised that he knew the robber and driver who wore no mask. It was I.

For a time Nigel and I had worked at the same dental practice in the Kensington area. He was a dental nurse but left a couple of years ago when he became tired of dentistry and of city life. We kept in touch for a while and so I knew that he had moved to Cornwall where he hoped to set up his own business. Technology was his new venture but then he had always been that way inclined.

When Nigel realised it was I in the picture he decided that rather than go to the police he would demand a share of the money raised from the sale of the jewellery and so blackmailed the four of us. We paid him fifty thousand pounds for his silence and hoped that was the end of it.

After that the months slipped by, we heard nothing more until we were alerted by Julian, one of our gang who now lives in Cornwall, that Nigel Taylor had had a heart attack and died. On hearing this news we were worried that copies of the pictures Nigel had taken might still be on his phone or his laptop and so Julian was instructed to break into the house in Hawthorn Road where we hoped he might retrieve both items. Julian, however, was unwilling to go there alone and so another member of our gang who was in Cornwall incognito agreed to go with him. What we didn't realise though was that Nigel's erstwhile landlady, Vivien Spencer, was staying there to oversee the house's refurbishment following his demise. As you've already guessed she surprised our duo, they panicked and sadly she paid with her life. But please believe me, it was an accident. Murder is something we all abhor. But Julian panicked. He thought she might scream and alert the neighbours and so he grabbed a cushion and held it over her face to muffle her cry. When she stopped struggling he thought that she was ready to comply with his commands but the real reason was that she was dead. Julian I can say hand on heart was devastated.

Initially of course, when the police heard about the money in the vacuum cleaner they concluded that was what our team had been after and because it wasn't there for the taking the police assumed the laptop and phone were taken rather than us leave empty handed. It seems, however, that poor Vivien died in vain. Pictures taken after the robbery were not on either device for Nigel had cunningly deleted them. Disappointed that our mission was unsuccessful, we knew it was possible that our identity might be revealed for Nigel had told us that he had copies of the pictures should anything untoward happen to him and for that reason after the police had finished their investigations we knew we had to resume our search of the house in Hawthorn Road.

During the time we worked together I learned that Nigel was a great one for teasing and loved puzzles and as I scratched my head thinking where the pictures might be hidden I recalled the message he sent to us telling of the copies in which he gave three clues as to their whereabouts. I scrolled through my phone and found the message in question. The first clue was 'It's an open and shut case'. I knew it couldn't refer to his laptop because we'd already checked and so that stumped me. The second was 'I've got you covered' and the third was 'You'll be going round in circles'. After much deliberation I concluded the second might refer to the cover of a book.

Meanwhile, one of us four, Craig Western, a young junior reporter who writes for one for one of the tabloids, was encouraged by our gang leader to get a story from you both about the money in the vacuum cleaner for his newspaper. That same day I was also travelling down from Kensington to

Cornwall, my mission to keep my ears open for anything that might tell us where the pictures could be hidden and if possible I would go to the house and search through any books there to seek the vital clue.

Craig was a little nervous about conducting an interview with you both although he agreed it seemed the logical way to ascertain any little clue that might lead us to the pictures. Sadly when he phoned in to report how the meeting had gone, our leader felt that he could no longer be trusted. Craig liked you both and said with relish what lovely ladies you were and how you fed him cheese on toast with onions. Of course when the news was relayed to me, I had no idea that the lovely ladies were you, Henrietta and Charlotte. It wasn't until I met you in the Crown and Anchor that I realised. Please believe me when I say that I was genuinely shocked, and I was shocked even more when I heard that Craig had decided to stay in Cornwall for the weekend. This caused our leader who was lying low in Newquay to panic and drive to Penzance, stalk him and wait for the opportunity to run him down hoping by doing so it would look like a simple case of hit and run. The reason for this was that if Craig were to meet up with anyone who knew either Nigel Taylor or Vivien Spencer then he might inadvertently let slip something incriminating.

That left just the three of us to search for the pictures and our hopes were pinned on finding them inside a book. In desperation, Julian went back to the house to have another look and on that occasion I went with him but of course we found nothing. There was a bookcase in the house but it was empty. And then one day, Henrietta we learned the reason why and we thought our luck had changed. The reason being when you showed me around your beautiful home you mentioned that some of the books in the dining room had come from the house in Hawthorn Road. After leaving your home I promptly reported this to our leader, who then, delighted by my news, *along with Julian broke into your house hopeful of finding the pictures inside one of the books. We chose a Tuesday for the search because you told me that you played bingo then and always went to the pub afterwards. Such a shame that you came home early that night and curtailed their search before they found what they were looking for. And then in the end it was you and the police who found the pictures and on a compact disc of all places but that no doubt was the 'going around in circles' referred to by Nigel as well as 'the open and shut case'.*

I had of course gone home prior to the break-in for we decided that I had been in the village quite long enough and that if I were no longer around when your house was burgled then fingers would not be pointed at me. After all I knew about the books because you told me and therefore I might have become a suspect.

For what it's worth, the four members of our gang, are, of course, me, Craig Western, who I pray makes a full recovery, Julian Digsby, my dear godson who you know as Jay, and our leader none other than your arch-enemy, Peggy Piggott or as you called her Peggy Piggy-eyes.

And so there it is. To say I wish I could turn back the clock would be an understatement. And I don't mean turning it back to the days before the robbery, I mean turning it back to the nineteen seventies and the day I left you, Henrietta for Peggy. I was a fool but as it is I'm a crooked fool and you're better off without me.

I am of course now back in London but not my home in Kensington. I have been arrested, charged and now await my fate. Peggy and Julian are also here under lock and key. Craig Western has been moved and is now in hospital here in the City. He has regained consciousness and will be arrested if and when he is well enough.

Your DI Fox has very kindly allowed me to unburden myself. At the same time he is pleased that you should learn the truth. You've had a rough ordeal and for that I am truly sorry. Had I known at the outset that our felonious ways might one day affect you, Henrietta then I never, never would have participated.

And for the record as I said when we met again after all these years, Peggy and I did not marry but we were reunited five years ago when she moved to Surrey. It was she who dreamt up the plan for the robbery (there were others too) and I being a fool fell for the glamour of it all. Money was never my objective.

I hope you find it in your hearts to forgive me.

Love,
Charles. X

When Lottie finished and folded the sheet of paper she saw that all three ladies were wiping their eyes.

"I don't know what to say, Het," sobbed Debbie, "I don't know whether to say you've had a lucky escape or what. I mean, I really thought when Charles first arrived on the scene that you might have rekindled your relationship and who knows what might have happened."

Hetty shook her head. "It's alright, Debbie and please don't weep for me. I've learned a lot from this experience and I would never have left you all for Charles or anyone else. This is my home now. It's where I belong and where I intend to stay. Besides, Charles and I were never meant to be. I know that now."

"But you've been treated so badly," said Kitty.

"No, I've lost nothing but perhaps a little pride whereas poor Polly has lost a husband, albeit a no-good husband, and she is left with a great void in her life."

Chapter Twenty-Four

Polly Digsby was devastated when she was told of her husband's arrest and involvement regarding the murder of Vivien Spencer and the jewellery shop robbery which had taken place before they had moved to Cornwall. They had separate bank accounts and she had always assumed the money he had to spend and to buy the house with was from the sales of his art work. As she looked through tear-stained eyes at his painting of a sunset over the sea she realised that she had been a gullible fool. Surely no-one in their right mind would pay good money for a talentless so-called work of art such as that. Angered by his deceit she reached up to take the painting from the wall but to her surprise found she could not remove it, for memories of hanging it in late October when they had moved into the house caused her to pause; they had been so happy that day; they loved their new home and looked forward to making a success of their new life together in Cornwall. How could things have gone so horribly wrong? As tears again welled in her eyes she sat back down and considered the days, weeks and years that lay ahead. For following Jay's arrest, the airline company for whom she worked had given her unlimited compassionate leave and insisted she take her time to decide upon her future.

Norman, on hearing of his neighbour's arrest, realised that the evening on which he'd looked after Barnaby was the evening when Jay and someone called Peggy something or other had broken into Primrose Cottage. Riddled with guilt he called on Polly the following day and told her that he would do everything he could to help her and that included looking after Barnaby if she chose to return to work doing a job he knew she loved. Jackie said likewise and so did everyone else in Cobblestone Close and beyond. Polly, overcome with emotion, thanked everyone for their kindness and said that she very much hoped to return to work eventually when the wound had healed a little.

Julian Digsby was angry. Angry that he and his colleagues had been found out. Angry with Vivien Spencer for being in the house in Hawthorn Road when they thought no-one was there. And angry with Nigel Taylor for dying on the day he went away up-country for a two-week Christmas break with Polly. For had he known sooner, one of their gang could have broken into number thirteen over the Christmas period confident that the house would be empty. He was also angry with the sisters who returned home early to Primrose Cottage and found them in their house before they had a chance to find the sought-after book. But most of all, he was angry with himself for getting involved in the first place, and for that he firmly placed the blame on his godfather, Charles Rowlett.

Charles was a friend of Julian's late father and they had been friends since their schooldays. However, after the birth of Julian, Julian's parents had moved away and so the friendship faded. Nevertheless, Charles remained a devoted godfather and never forgot Julian's birthday or failed to send him a gift at Christmas. It was when Charles learned that Julian was struggling to make ends meet as an artist that Charles had offered him the chance of making some serious money, albeit illegally. Julian, eager to settle down with his long-term girlfriend, Polly, readily agreed and after a couple of robberies he felt financially secure and asked her to marry him. She agreed, they married and when Julian suggested they buy a house in Cornwall, she jumped at the idea, little knowing that Pentrillick was the choice of Peggy Piggott who wanted Julian in the area to keep an eye on Nigel Taylor.

Peggy Piggott kicked the wall of her cell. She was furious. Furious because Julian had foolishly killed Vivien Spencer and thus condemned them all through association. Furious that Charles had mistimed the hour at which the twin sisters would return home from the pub on the night she and Julian had broken into their house thus thwarting their attempts to find the incriminating evidence. Furious that Craig had taken a liking to said sisters who had fed him cheese on toast and had given him two thimbles. But most of all she was furious with the twin sisters themselves. For were it not for their interfering all would have gone to plan. For not only had they managed to get the vacuum cleaner and its contents but they had ended up with the compact disc holding pictures of the get-away including one of Charles who had stupidly not kept his face hidden in the first place.

Peggy paced the small room. She knew back in the seventies when she began her career as a fresh faced journalist that Henrietta Tonkins was trouble, for it had taken a lot of effort to prise Charles away from her, but at least she got him in the end not that she really wanted him. In fact she was beginning to wish she had never set eyes on him. And now those awful twins had got the better of her. They were free, happy and local heroes whereas she was likely to spend a good many years, probably even the rest of her life, behind bars for robbery and the attempted murder of Craig Western. Bah humbug! There was no justice in the world.

As he lay in a hospital bed, Craig Western, weak, battered and bruised, had plenty of time to think about the events of the past five years and reflect on how much he wished he could turn back the clock. However, where he would like to turn back the clock to he was unsure. In fact the more he thought about it the more he wondered how he had ever come under the spell of Peggy Piggott in the first place. She was years older than him so perhaps he had seen her as a mother figure or even a grandmother figure.

They had first met five years earlier at a police press conference where details were released of a serious armed bank robbery in the City. Most of the reporters there had been appalled by the brutality of the gang but not Peggy; she saw it as glamorous and as time went by she realised that she could make a lot more money as a criminal than she ever would as a crime reporter. Furthermore, she felt that writing of unlawful acts for many years had given her a glimpse as to how things worked in the criminal underworld.

Peggy handpicked her associates with care and Craig knew that he had been chosen because he looked a picture of innocence and it was unlikely anyone would ever suspect him of robbery. To help keep him under her wing, Peggy secured him a job as a junior crime reporter on the newspaper where she was departmental head.

Craig leaned forwards and reached for the beaker of water on the cabinet beside his bed. Careful not to disturb the wires and tubes attached to his body he took a sip, then laid back his head and thought of Cornwall. When he had first recovered consciousness after the accident he was unable to remember anything and then slowly it all came back. He remembered two dear ladies with a vacuum cleaner, a hotel room with sea views and buying thimbles in charity shops. His last memory was taking part in a quiz by the fire in a pub with one if its regulars. After that everything was blank but the previous memories were sweet and he recalled them with great pleasure until he learned through questioning by the police that he had been knocked down deliberately by Peggy Piggott in a hit and run and that the whole gang were under arrest.

Craig thought of his future. He was glad that his days of being a criminal were over and he knew that the long years ahead looked bleak. For without doubt he faced a long stretch in prison. But he was young, not yet thirty and he vowed that to keep himself sane he would be a model prisoner with a goal that on his release he would return to Cornwall and begin a new life there.

Graham Spencer stood by the picture windows of his Devonshire home and looked out to sea. The police had just left having called to tell him the latest news regarding the death of his wife, Vivien. Graham was in a state of shock. Shock, because a man he thought to be a friend, was actually involved with the persons who had taken the life of his beloved wife. A man who had offered his condolences and seemed sincere in his expressions of sympathy had known all along who was to blame and why. Graham felt deeply saddened. How could Charles Rowlett have behaved in such an unscrupulous manner?

Charles Rowlett blamed no-one for his misfortune. He had chosen his path in life with care and exactitude and had no complaints. Admittedly he regretted that Vivien Spencer had died and had great sympathy for her widower whose company he had enjoyed enormously during his stay in Pentrillick. And while Vivien should still be alive and enjoying life he knew that her death was not his doing and therefore he felt only a little guilt.

Charles wondered if he would ever be a free man again. He was seventy years of age and because of Vivien's death and the attempted murder of Craig it was likely that all four would receive heavy sentences even though not all four were involved with the individual crimes.

As he sat and pondered his bleak future he looked back to the past and the early nineteen seventies when he and Henrietta were deemed the perfect couple. It was assumed by all that marriage was inevitable; he even thought so himself but Peggy had lured him away and perhaps because of the villainous streak in his character, parting with Henrietta was for the best.

A week after the arrest of Charles, Peggy, and Julian, Hetty told Lottie that she going to Marazion on the bus and from there she intended to take the coastal path to Penzance. Lottie knew by her sister's face that it was not necessary to offer herself as company for it was obvious that Hetty needed to be alone and the coastal path was one of her favourite walks. For since receiving the letter from Charles, Hetty had become withdrawn and Lottie longed to see her sister back to her old self.

A fresh wind blew as Hetty stepped from the bus. She pulled up the collar of her coat, tightened her scarf and put on a pair of woollen gloves. With hands deep in pockets she then walked along the path, onto the beach, over the sand dunes and across stepping stones sporadically placed in the shallow water of a stream. When she reached steps she climbed up from the sand and onto the path which ran between the sea and the railway track. Being a weekday, the path was quiet and she saw only a few dog walkers, joggers, and the occasional cyclist.

The grey sea, its waves whipped up by the wind, looked wild, cold and unwelcoming; devoid of human life it lapped around Saint Michaels' Mount: where the castle and medieval church on its peak loomed eerily beneath the leaden sky. Hetty walked briskly and with care, frequently glancing at the path to avoid treading in puddles left by recent rain. When a train passed by she stopped and watched. It was one of the new green trains which she assumed was en route for London. Instinctively she blew a kiss and said it was for Charles.

After passing the level crossing at Long Rock she clambered down onto the beach; the tide was going out and so she walked for a while on the hard, wet, compressed sand. A few gulls kept her company and a small dog rushed by chasing a stick thrown by a young woman with an energetic toddler.

As she neared Penzance, Hetty left the sand, sat to rest on one of the many boulders and watched the sea as it splashed and tumbled onto the long stretch of shore. The repetitiveness of the sound and motion she felt helped to clear her head and relieve tension built up since she and Lottie had received the upsetting letter from Charles.

The path ended in Penzance near to the bus and railway stations. From there she strolled through the town until she reached a familiar turning where she left the main street and walked until she reached the junction by Wesley Road. As she stood outside the Nag's Head she peered in through the window. Reg Whittle the landlord was not behind the bar. The person on duty was a woman. Nervously Hetty went inside. It was early for lunchtime drinkers and so very few people sat around the tables and no-one was on the barstools.

Hetty approached the bar. "Is Reg around, please?" she asked.

"No, day off, love. Can I help?"

"Oh, yes, yes, you can." From her pocket, Hetty pulled an envelope. "Would you or Reg give this to Don please when next you see him?"

"Will that be Don Pascoe?"

"Probably. I don't know his surname but he told me that he used to be a friend of Nigel Taylor and they played dominos together."

"Yes, that'd be Don Pascoe then." The barmaid took the envelope. There was nothing written on it other than the name Don.

"It's an explanation," said Hetty, feeling that she ought to explain, "about Nigel's death. I thought it only fair that Don should know what it was that had been bothering his friend. Hopefully it'll give him peace of mind. It also says a little about Craig Western. You know, the young man in the hit and run who'd done the quiz with Don."

"I see. I assume you know Don then and knew Nigel too."

"Yes. No. That is I never knew Nigel even though I live in Pentrillick and I only saw Don once when I was in for a drink with friends. That's when I spoke to him and he told me a bit about Nigel."

"Okay. Well anyway, I'll make sure he gets it." The barmaid tucked the envelope beside the till.

"Thank you."

As Hetty turned to leave the barmaid called after her. "I was here that night working so I saw that chap Craig," she spoke with sadness, "He was ever so nice; sweet and chatty and we were all really upset when we heard what had happened to him. I've heard rumours saying they've got the person who ran him down but I don't know whether or not it's true."

"Yes, it's true. Someone has been arrested and charged. And you're right, Craig was nice but sadly he took a wrong path in life and it nearly cost him his life."

The barmaid's eyebrows rose.

Hetty pointed to the letter. "I'm sure once he's read it Don will explain it to you all but it's not something I want to talk about at the moment."

Aware that Hetty's voice trembled as she spoke, the barmaid knew it was time to curb her inquisitiveness. "Fair enough and on Don's behalf I'll say thank you."

"You're welcome."

Hetty felt a sense of relief as she left the Nag's Head but by the junction she paused. There was no sign of the hit and run and for that she was grateful. With a heavy heart she strolled back through the town. As she reached the bus station she saw there were a few raindrops on the pavement and the sky looked even more threatening. Rather than walk back to Marazion along the coastal path, she decided to wait in Penzance and from there catch the next bus back to Pentrillick.

Chapter Twenty-Five

As February drew to a close, the village's woeful news story was still the main topic of conversation, although many residents, heartened by the occasional appearance of the sun between frequent heavy showers and gale force winds, optimistically tried to move on and looked forward to the spring; especially gardeners whose enthusiasm was boosted by preparations for the village's second Pentrillick in Bloom competition.

In Hawthorn Road, Susan and Tim Rudd who lived in the house next door to number thirteen, were in the throes of exposing their bricked-up fireplace. For frequently, when Oscar was not in their garden and failed to come home when called, Susan by peeping through the living room window of the unoccupied house, had discovered him sitting on the cold carpetless floor beside the empty grate. On each occasion she had tapped on the glass to attract his attention and he left by way of the cat flap, but when he came home, she always sensed an air of melancholy. Feeling sorry for the cat, Susan suggested to Tim that they open up the fireplace and install a log burning stove. Tim wholeheartedly agreed, for since he had retired he spent more time at home and liked the idea of a focal point in their sitting room other than the television set.

On the very last day of February, Zac awoke at ten past seven to find Emma was already up, so he gathered his clothes, went to the bathroom for a shower, then downstairs for breakfast. It was still quite dark for the morning was overcast and so lights needed to be on, but nevertheless when he walked into the kitchen he was surprised to see scented candles flickering on the table and the curtains still drawn.

"Have we had a power cut?" He glanced around and then answered his own question, "No, we can't have because the light's on in the hallway." He cast a questioning glance at Emma who appeared to be nervous. "Are you alright, Em? Your hands are shaking."

"Yes, yes, of course I am. Please sit down, Zac."

"Why? What's wrong? And why the candles? They smell lovely but it's breakfast time for goodness sake."

She attempted to smile but found it difficult. "Nothing's wrong and the candles are to create a romantic atmosphere."

"Romantic atmosphere? What over scrambled eggs?"

"Please, Zac, just sit down."

Feeling bewildered, he sat down heavily on the chair Emma had pulled out from beneath the table. Instantly she dropped down on one knee in front of him and took his hands in hers. "Zac, as you know it's Leap Year Day today which means that I as a female can umm…that is to say…I can ask. Oh damn it. Will you marry me, Zac?"

His jaw dropped, his eyes sparkled, and he began to laugh.

"Oh please say yes," she implored.

He leaned forwards and pulled her into his arms. "Yes, yes, of course I will."

Emma burst into tears. "I've been so worried because I thought you might say no."

"Why would I do that, you Muppet? I'm absolutely delighted. Thrilled to bits in fact. You see, I've been wanting to ask you ever since we moved here but I haven't been able to pluck up enough courage because I thought *you* might say no. In fact I thought of asking you on Valentine's Day and even went as far as looking at engagement rings in the jeweller's window but I didn't go in because I wasn't sure what you'd like and didn't know what size to get." He squeezed her tight, "But as we've nothing planned for today, shall we pop down to Penzance and go ring shopping?"

Emma took her tissue from her sleeve and dried her eyes. "Yes please, Zac, but first we must pass on our good news."

Before they ate breakfast, Zac and Emma rang their parents. Thereafter phones rang around the village and mobiles beeped with text messages. For Bill on hearing the news had phoned James at the Crown and Anchor to warn him there would be a spontaneous engagement party that evening and so the pub would be a little busier than a usual Saturday night in February. James, thrilled at the prospect of a busy night said that he and Ella would lay on a modest buffet at their own expense.

The evening was a huge success. The bar was packed and the overspill went into the dining room. Emma's ring was admired by every female, cards piled up on top of the piano, sixties music rang out from the speakers and dancing even broke out on the sun terrace despite the fact that it was cold out there.

After the party, Hetty, Lottie, Kitty and Tommy walked up Long Lane much as they had done two months before in fancy dress costumes on New Year's Eve. Strong to gale force winds blew from the west and the pitch-black sky obscured the stars and the waxing moon they had witnessed earlier when going down the hill en route to the Crown and Anchor.

"Such a lot has happened in the first two months of this year, I really can't keep up with it all," said Kitty, "Hopefully things will quieten down a bit now."

Lottie sighed. "I agree with you there. So far this year, poor Vivien has died, Craig has been knocked down and is seriously ill, three people we know are in prison and for several others, I'm thinking of Graham Spencer and poor Polly, their lives have changed forever."

Tommy wagged his finger. "And don't forget the dreadful flooding up-country and the coronavirus. They're of great concern as well."

"Oh yes they are. Both are dreadful and ongoing too," agreed Lottie, "Poor people. I'd hate to have our home flooded and as for the coronavirus I suppose it's inevitable that it'll worsen in this country and as we're in our late sixties we'll be considered at risk."

"Maybe, but at least we're all in good health," reasoned Kitty, "and that's something to be thankful for."

"Anyway," said Tommy, "going back to Craig Western, there's no need to worry about him now because he's out of danger. I heard on the radio just before we came out that they've got him out of bed and he now faces arrest."

Hetty tutted. "Silly, silly boy and now because of greed and the fact he was easily influenced he will spend the best years of his life under lock and key."

"Yes, he will and of all the four he's the only one that I have any sympathy for," said Lottie, "which is sad because I liked Jay."

Hetty attempted to push strands of hair from her face tousled by the wind. "So did I. At least I thought I did. Norman and Jackie got on well with him too. What a mess."

Kitty attempted to be positive. "Anyway, tomorrow sees the beginning of a new month and if we're all going to put on a good show along Blackberry Way we need to start thinking about sowing seeds and making plans for the Pentrillick in Bloom competition. I heard several people talking about it this evening and we don't want to get left behind."

Hetty actually smiled. "Well, we're all ready for that, Kitty and despite the weather we're really looking forward to the new series of *Gardeners' World*. As for the competition, we bought seeds and compost the other day and they're in the garage ready and awaiting our attention."

"And who knows. We might have a wedding to attend before the year is out," said Lottie, excitedly, "So we'll need plenty of flowers for that occasion."

"How wonderful," gushed Kitty, "You can't beat a good wedding."

"Damn right, and you can wear your vintage frock, Het," laughed Lottie.

"Yes, I suppose I could. After all it's in excellent condition and the colour suits me."

"Do you think they'll get married this year then?" Kitty asked.

"I don't see why not, after all they have a house to live in and they are devoted to each other," said Lottie, "and Sandra told me the twins have already been asked to be bridesmaids along with Emma's little sister, Claire."

Hetty nodded. "And I heard Zac telling Jackie that he's asked his old school friend, Dodge to be his best man and that Dodge said he'd be delighted and looks forward to partying in Cornwall again."

Lottie gasped. "And I've just realised: Barbara is sure to come over from the States for her nephew's wedding, so we'll be able to meet the new boyfriend we've heard so much about. If she brings him with her, that is."

"What's his name again?" Hetty asked.

"Jed something or other. I can't remember his surname. I know he's a police officer though so if he comes over we'll have to be on our best behaviour."

Kitty clapped her hands with glee. "That'll be fun. And of course if Zac and Emma get married this summer they'll be the first couple Vicar Sam will marry since he got married himself."

"And with Emma being events' manager at Pentrillick House they're bound to have the reception there so it would almost be a rerun," enthused Lottie.

"What'll happen to the money?" Tommy suddenly asked.

"Money?" Kitty queried, "What money?"

"The fifty thousand."

Kitty tutted. "Trust you to think of that, Tommy Thomas."

"I'd not given it any more thought," confessed Hetty, "Does anybody know?"

"Probably go to the jewellers," reasoned Lottie, "part compensation for their loss."

"But surely the insurance will have reimbursed that," said Kitty.

"Yes, I suppose it would. I don't know then and can't even make another guess."

"And I'd rather not think about it or where Nigel got it from," sighed Hetty, "It's history now and best forgotten."

"I agree and so back to a more cheerful note. Has anyone heard anything more about the prospective purchaser of number thirteen Hawthorn Road?" Lottie asked, "I should love to know who it is."

Kitty's face lit up. "Oh yes, I knew there was something I needed to tell you but with one thing and another it slipped my mind. My brain's like a sieve these days, you know."

Lottie laughed when Kitty failed to divulge the name. "So who is it?"

"What? Oh, yes, sorry. It's James and Ella."

"What James and Ella from the pub?" Lottie was taken aback.

"Well of course. How many James and Ellas do you know?"

"Yeah, okay they're the only ones but why would they want a house in Hawthorn Road when they have perfectly nice accommodation in the pub?"

"Apparently because they love the village and love the pub but at the same time they want somewhere to go when they have a day off and because of the recent happenings, the house was quite a snip. It's said that Graham Spencer is thrilled they're buying it because they were very good to him when he was here, and James and Ella are keen to get the sale over and done with quickly for his sake so it severs all ties the poor man had with the village."

At the top of Long Lane they turned into Blackberry Way and outside Primrose Cottage they wished each other goodnight. Kitty and Tommy then walked briskly on towards their home at the end of the lane.

"It's nice to get in out of that wind," said Hetty, as she locked the front door and switched off the outside light.

"It is." Lottie headed straight for the kitchen and picked up the kettle. "Fancy a coffee, Het? I'm having one."

"Yes, thanks, I think I will. My throat feels a bit hoarse having had to shout to make ourselves heard over the noise in the pub and my hands are cold too so I can warm them on the mug."

Both sisters removed their coats and Hetty hung them on pegs in the hallway.

"You've seemed a bit subdued tonight, Het," Lottie placed two mugs on the work surface and spooned coffee granules into them, "I hope you're not sickening for something."

Hetty smiled as she pulled out a chair from under the kitchen table. "You sound like our mother."

"Yes, I suppose I do," chuckled Lottie, "It's funny how we turn into our parents, isn't it?"

"Hmm, but not surprising."

Lottie placed the mugs of coffee on the table and then sat down opposite her sister. "If you don't mind me saying so I think you've been awfully brave, Het. These last few weeks can't have been easy for you and then on top of that there's all the talk of weddings."

"I don't begrudge Zac and Emma their happiness, Lottie, and I think it was a lovely idea of Emma's to ask Zac to marry her on Leap Year Day. It's good to see him laughing again too after the Hawthorn Road discovery. Poor lad. That must have been very hard for him. And yes, you're right, I have struggled a bit lately I must admit but I can see the light at the end of the tunnel now."

"Promise?"

"Yes, I promise."

"Well, if there's anything I can do please don't hesitate to ask."

"I know that and thank you but there's nothing you can do, Lottie. What's done is done and only time can heal it. Anyway, as Kitty said tomorrow is the beginning of another month. What's more spring is just around the corner. The daffodils are in full bloom, lots of primroses are out and we have much to be thankful for. We have our health, Lottie. Good friends and family and you had a very happy marriage and I know that Hugh would be proud of the way you have coped since his passing."

After they finished their coffee, the sisters made their way to bed each clutching a hot water bottle. On the upstairs landing they wished each other goodnight and went to their respective rooms.

The church clock struck one, as Hetty changed into her nightdress and then brushed her hair. As she placed her best shoes in the bottom of the wardrobe, she spotted the dress she had purchased from the vintage clothes stall in the village hall. She took it from the rack and held it in front of herself; sweet memories flooded back as she looked at her reflection in the full length mirror. With a deep sigh she hung the dress back in the wardrobe and closed the door. But before she snuggled down beneath the duvet she sat on the floor and opened the bottom drawer of her dressing table. From it she took a large book; her diary for 1976. Carefully she opened it on the month of February and took from between the pages a sizable coloured photograph in a plastic sleeve. The photograph was of herself and Charles and was taken at the wedding of a mutual friend. In it, Hetty was wearing the identical dress to the newly acquired one in her wardrobe. She removed the picture from its sleeve and dropped the sleeve onto the floor. The picture she turned over. On its back Charles had written: *Our turn next, my darling. You looked stunning in that dress...Love always and forever, Charles xxxxxx.* It was dated February 29th 1976.

Hetty placed the diary minus the picture back inside the drawer. She then stood and with picture in hand quietly left her room and crept down the stairs. From the hallway she gently opened the door of the sitting room and slipped inside. In front of the stove she knelt on the hearth rug and opened the glass door. With one last look she stroked and then kissed the image of Charles. She then tossed the photograph into the dying embers, closed the door and watched as the picture blackened and curled, burst into flames and then crumbled into the ash.

THE END

Printed in Great Britain
by Amazon